THE WORD PARTY

an anthology of short stories
from the MA in Creative Writing
at the University of East Anglia

Centre for Creative and Performing Arts

Published by the Centre for Creative and Performing Arts, The University of East Anglia, Norwich.

Printed and bound by Billing & Sons Limited, Worcester.

Set in Linotype Goudy Old Face

British Library Cataloguing in Publication Data

The Word Party.
   I. Bowker, Peter, 1959-
   II. Centre for Creative and Performing Arts
   823.0108 [FS]

ISBN 0-9515009-2-9

acknowledgements

The editors would like to thank the following for their help and advice: Dominic Belisario, Jane Chittenden, Jon Cook, Eastern Arts Association, The Norfolk Institute of Art and Design, Mike Oakes, Phoebe Phillips, Peter Tombs, Anastacia Tohill and Andy Vargo.

The Word Party is edited by Peter Bowker, Glyn Brown, Francis Gilbert and Erica Wagner.

contents

❖

❖

INTRODUCTION
Malcolm Bradbury

This is now the third in line of the anthologies of new fiction that have come out of the MA in Creative Writing at the University of East Anglia. In fact, these volumes are already beginning to feel like a heritage or tradition. The two earlier collections, *Unthank* and *Exposure*, came from the work of the writers who took the course in the two years previous to this one, and they seem already to have proved their worth, at least to the extent that several of the writers in them have either published or are just about to publish their own independent volumes of fiction. I can only hope that the same is about to happen to the thirteen writers in the present collection, whose work is in the pages that follow.

The purpose of an introduction is to introduce, and there are a few things that should be said. One is that (once again) the writers who took the course in 1990 – 91 were a very international group – British, Irish, American, Australian, Indian – and their work therefore displays the cultural diversity that is increasingly characteristic of contemporary writing. Another is that a number of them are already published writers, journalists or film-makers, whose main work is not necessarily in the form of the short story, in which they exhibit themselves here. The stories they have produced are various enough to make it hard for me to generalize, though one thing about them does strike me. One is that few of the stories are in any obvious sense political, a reflection, perhaps, of the mood that still survives from the Eighties. Indeed, the larger historical and ideological situation of our times – the fading of the Cold War, the realignment of Europe, the growing feelings of historical instability and uncertainty – does not generally enter into these pieces. Many of the stories are set in that half-timeless and semi-personal world of the near present in which a good deal of modern fiction seems to be located. Of course, the real politics within fiction often lies in its more subtle details: in the shifting spirit of moral expectation, in the changing form of gender or generational relations, in the degree of romance or irony, of hope or of doubt, in which our tales are told. With some interesting exceptions (the stories of Suzanne Cleminshaw, Judith Condon or Leena Dhingra, for example), most of these stories are about personal rather than general politics, aspects of private rather than public history.

This may reflect something about the nature of the short story itself, a form of subtle perspective and of natural intensity, often set around one single and concentrated moment. I like the way in which several of these stories – Peter Bowker's, Glyn Brown's, Erica Wagner's – work by contrast, breaking up the central moment into fragments. I like the wry and deliberately understated economy of the two brief pieces by Robert Cremins and Clare Morgan, both of whom often write in much larger forms. I am, incidentally, not too sure whether to be glad or sorry that this volume contains the first story from the creative writing workshop to be about a creative writing workshop, though John Mangan's 'The Ambassador,' though it is based on a certain amount of truth, is rightly based on quite a lot more fiction. But the reader will soon find that this volume does what a volume of short stores surely ought to do – that is, illustrates the form as one of considerable variety, one that ranges from the well-rounded tale to the story of subtle impression, from the public and social story to, as in Francis Gilbert's, the intense and personal fantasy. Once again it would be impossible to say that the writers here form a particular school or tendency, though they do have in common a seriousness that has been honed over a very co-operative and supportive year.

But one thing they *do* have in common is that they took the creative writing course in 1990 – 91, the year in which, as it happens, it celebrates its twentieth year of existence. As such occasions do, this one produced among those involved in the teaching of the course (Rose Tremain, Jon Cook and myself) a certain amount of analytical retrospect, otherwise known as taking stock. Planning a reunion, we discovered that something like 100 writers had taken the course over those twenty years. We were also pleased to discover that about a third of them were now regularly publishing authors. The first of them all was, of course, Ian McEwan, who flew the pilot year solo, and convinced all involved that if there were writers of this calibre to take the programme it must truly be worthwhile.

Since then, there have been good years and bad, moments of great confidence and moments of doubt. During the 1970's it often seemed that it was hard for even the genuinely good writers to get published, but then we had the reassurance of seeing two members of the group, Clive Sinclair and Kazuo Ishiguro, make their way to distinction. What has since emerged is that many of the writers who began in the course at that time – I think of Dave Peak, James Sorel-Cameron and Paul Stewart – have, if more slowly, made their way into well-deserved notice; a literary career is often a slow, hard affair. The 1980's happily saw greater opportunities in Britain for new writers, and with that came a refreshing and vigorous era in British fiction. And this was very happily reflected in the way many of the best authors on the course – including Louise Doughty, Susannah Dunn, Mark Illis, Dierdre Madden, Kathy Page, Glenn Patterson, David Rose – quickly made their way to well-deserved attention.

So to the nineties. The turn-of-the-century decade has simultaneously begun with a spirit of unprecedented change and of gloomy recession. The sense of change means that the perspective and vision of the new generation of writers are that much more necessary for the interpretation of our times. The recession brings a spirit of retrenchment among publishers, doubt among booksellers, caution among readers. It would be truly dismaying if the new energies that have been released in recent fiction were not to find publishers and audiences, but I believe they will. I am certain that among those new writers will be several of the names whose work you are about to read.

KEEPING TIME

Peter Bowker

I sacked Ted again this evening. He's been getting on my nerves for forty years so I feel I've been more than generous. If he's looking for somebody to blame then he need look no further than Glenn Miller.

We were playing 'In The Mood' when a woman smiled at me. I'm in showbusiness so naturally I'm used to this kind of attention but then at 68 it doesn't happen as often as it used to. I had noticed her earlier in the evening. She and her partner had done a passable rhumba with back breaker turns during our Latin American medley. She was wearing a petrol blue dress with gold shoes and matching gold purse. She checked the contents of the purse every few minutes, breaking off dancing to do it, her partner tapping his foot in time to the music so they could resume without missing a beat.

After 'In The Mood' I announced a break because Frank – tenor sax – wanted to phone his wife in Rochdale. The brass section raced over to the bar, with the woodwind in hot pursuit.

I was mopping the back of my neck with a bar towel when the woman approached me, the one who had been smiling.

"Hello," she said.

"Good evening madam," I replied.

She let her right hand fall to her purse and began to fiddle with the clasp. I surveyed her nervous smile, her heavy lidded eyes and her comical chin. I felt the damp towel I was holding tickling my fingers.

"You don't remember me, do you?" she said.

"Pardon?"

"You don't remember me."

"Blackpool Tower Ballroom? 1986?"

The woman shook her head, then rather than enlighten me went on, "Your band plays very well. Very suitable, very appropriate. Waltz, waltz, foxtrot. Waltz, waltz, quickstep."

She glanced at the rows of music stands and discarded instruments as she spoke and I wasn't sure if she was making fun of me or not. I didn't know that the programme of dances was so transparent, but when most of the dancers were the wrong side of fifty you had to pace them. I didn't want a row of ambulances waiting outside in the taxi rank.

I stared over at the bar and watched throats draining glasses and hands hastily reaching for a second. The trumpet players were crowding round our young drummer, Melanie. She was a round shouldered anaemic looking girl who smiled reluctantly at their tales of when they were jazz legends. A blue layer of cigarette smoke hung above them like thunder clouds.

"Wythenshaw Forum? 1970?"

The woman shook her head again and walked back to the table. She said something to her husband and he glanced over at me before drinking from his pint glass. I gestured over to the bar and a trail of red-eyed artistes in beer stained tuxedos staggered back to the stage. They looked like something David Attenborough should be following round.

"One. . . two. . . one, two, three, four."

I wielded my baton and we launched into 'Take The A Train'

and even though it was a bit messy – what with the brass section swapping instruments and hiding the trombonist's false teeth – I could sense the pleasure on the dance floor behind me. In between the throbs of music I could just make out the shoes tapping and sliding on the wooden tiles, the swirl of the nylon mix dresses. I could sense the couples turning in tidy circles, laughing and chatting, their limbs on automatic. I didn't look but I imagined the eyes of that woman were watching me.

We were into the middle eight and Ged – who is given to pushing back the boundaries of jazz – had nearly fallen off his piano stool chasing a note down the keyboard. We were into the middle eight and I was thinking that's the last time I give Ged a solo when I remembered where I'd seen her before. I was so pleased with myself that it must have showed through to the band because they started to play with a bit more spice.

✦

Early in 1948 our singer Elsie announced that she was pregnant. The father was Tom, the vibes player, which was something of a surprise as he couldn't normally keep a rhythm up to save his life.

It was very bad timing. We had been booked to play a six month cruise on an ocean liner and had to get a singer within the week. We even auditioned on a Monday, a day I normally put to one side to shake off Saturday's drink and Sunday's reprisals. I managed to borrow a room above a pub I knew. It was full of old crates and broken furniture which the boys had to drag to one side before setting up. The light was partially banished by thin blackout curtains and the smell was of old beer and dust. A stream of singers passed through that room but not one of them fitted the bill. We needed a girl who could sing, obviously, but she had to look a certain way. Nothing too sultry, nothing too showy, nothing that would get husband and wife arguing back in their luxury cabin. The band was getting restless and Ted wasn't helping matters. He was wearing a bow tie on a strip of elastic. Every so often he let his fingers stray from the neck of the double bass on to his throat then he'd pull the bow tie out until the elastic was straining and snap it back against his Adam's apple. Every time he did it the band fell about and the singer would think it was something she had done.

By dinner time I had filled an ashtray and an address book when a young girl turned up and sang, 'Take Me Right Back To The Track, Jack' and 'Don't Get Around Much Anymore'. Her voice never faltered. It was a good voice, it sounded a bit American but not too much and you could hear the Manchester accent breaking through. She seemed to understand instinctively what fitted with the rest of the band. And they seemed transformed by her. They actually swung, together, and you could hear that undertow you get with the really good outfits.

Even Ted stopped pissing about. All the cheeky chappy winks and glances were dispensed with and he concentrated all his energies on playing for once. Best of all, this young singer looked like a child, not a hint of sleaze about her. She wouldn't even meet your eye, her nails were bitten down to the finger ends.

"How old are you, love?" I had to ask her.

"Twenty."

I believed her. The war had made a lot of youngsters that way. Not enough greens, they never filled out properly. The streets were full of pale skinny grown-ups who looked like children still fuddled by sleep.

"Does your mother know you're here?"

"She sent me."

"She in the business herself?"

"She's a singer too."

"Who with?"

"The Victory V's."

"The Victory V's? So you're Edna Brownlow's daughter?"

The girl nodded. The Victory V's were a women's swing band who'd been a great hit on the American bases during the war. "I used to sing with them too sometimes."

"How did you like that?"

"Not much," she looked down at her shoes, "the G.I.'s were always asking me out. My mum had to put a stop to it."

The girl blushed and took a cigarette out of her handbag. She lit it herself, took one drag, then lodged it between her first and second fingers. She looked around, searching for somewhere to rest her eyes away from the band.

"Did you go out with them?" I asked, to kill the silence.

"No, no. Then," she laughed, "then they'd get rude and say I wouldn't go out with them because I was Jewish."

I nodded and frowned.

"But I'm not Jewish, you see. Do I look Jewish to you?"

I leaned back in my chair and looked at her dark hair and dark eyes. I blew my nose then rubbed at my shoes with the same handkerchief. Finally I said, "I don't go much on religion," and she seemed satisfied.

❖

After we got off the A Train we went on to grapple with 'Mack The Knife'. I glanced over my shoulder and smiled directly at

Joan Brownlow as she glided past in her husband's arms. The faces of the dancers were shining now and the smell of perfume and after-shave was cut through by alcohol and cigarettes. A dance has its own scent, its own climate, its own moth-eaten magic.

Melanie was holding 'Mack The Knife' together, and she needed to because Ged was at it again, adding those little flourishes that weren't anywhere in the original arrangement. Don't get me wrong. Ged knows his jazz. He's always on hand to tell me the latest twists and turns. The post-post bop, the new harmonics, fusion and all that other stuff that doesn't have a decent tune. He told me, for instance that 'Mack the Knife' was written by a communist.

"I don't care," I told him, "they've written some good tunes, those communists."

Just before we went into the chorus for the last time the stage lights caught the saxophones and shot out sharp blue reflections which hurt my eyes. My heart began to race and I managed to pop another tablet under my tongue before nodding Melanie in for a solo. She didn't make a bad job of it, a bit heavy on the hi-hat for my liking but I've yet to meet a drummer under the age of forty who can use the cymbals properly.

As I took the applause I waved Melanie up to share it. She rose slowly from behind her drum kit, dragging the hair out of her eyes. Polite applause rippled from the dance floor, there were even one or two whistles.

"Don't encourage her," I shouted, "she'll be wanting a pay rise."

I announced another break, stepped down from the stage and went over to talk to Joan Brownlow.

❖

On the first day of rehearsals she was at the stage door waiting for me. She looked even younger standing in the grey alley swinging her music bag. I had a bit of a struggle with the keys because they were newly cut. For rehearsals we used the space underneath the stage at the Garrick Theatre. I led the way and gestured for Joan to follow me into the long thin room. She did, and sat down in an old deck chair that had been left behind after some production. I tried not to stare at her, she was so small, pale scrawny calves coming out of white ankle socks, her big winter coat swamping her. She had a smudge of make-up on each cheek and was wearing red lipstick. She let her chin rest on the collar of her coat and swung her legs back and forth under the deck chair.

I switched all the lights on I could find and sang the refrain from a song I'd been writing. I'd got the melody straightened out but the words sounded all wrong. I could just imagine the snickering from behind the cornets when I handed the music sheets out. After fiddling with all the lights switches I sang my song again, louder this time, and closer to Joan.

"I've got something to tell you," she said, as I reached the chorus.

"Oh?" I stopped singing.

"Somebody has asked me to marry them. Not just somebody. A chap. My chap's asked me."

"Oh? And are congratulations in order?"

"I don't know. Depends."

"Do you love him?" My words hung above us like the steam from our breath.

"Yes."

"Well then."

I noticed that she had tiny flakes of lipstick on her teeth. I didn't say anything. I turned my back and imagined a stage across one wall with my band on it. Initials embroidered on the music stand covers. H.K. for Harry King, with a little crown logo above the K. 'Harry King's Bold As Brass.' I saw them all in white tuxedos, clean shaven boys who would respect me for the way I coaxed the best out of each of them. And the young singer I'd discovered – Joan Brownlow, a different name maybe, but the small girl with her sad voice. Singing of things she knew nothing about, but singing as though she understood. This cruise was just going to be the start. We'd go to the States, maybe Canada where my cousin had emigrated.

"He says he won't wait till I come back. He says he couldn't stand the thought of me and all those musicians."

"What?"

"He said, 'It's not fair. You meet the right girl then she runs off with a big band'."

I continued to stare at the wall. The rich image I had conjured up faded to a pale wash.

"You're not coming on the cruise then?"

There was a sob from behind me and I turned and saw Joan crying into her hands. I stood and watched before crouching next to her and offering a handkerchief. I tried to put my arms round her but the deck chair got in the way and I ended up clutching her head against my chest with my other hand resting on her hip. There was hair in my eyes and my mouth. Her cry was as surprising as her singing voice, you wouldn't have thought her lungs were up to it but she shook the room. I started to slowly rock her, nothing too extreme, just a gentle to and fro.

"Babies and marriages," I said, "hardly the jazz life is it?"

Things were calming down when Ted came in; her sobs were subsiding into little gasps. He was whistling as he negotiated his instrument case through the door but when he saw us he stopped abruptly. His eyes met mine and I saw how it must have looked. I let go of Joan and rose to my feet. She blinked up at me with pink eyes and I noticed a crimson mark on her cheek where she'd been pushed up against my jacket. We both watched Ted as he lovingly hung his new crombie on a nail on the wall and set about tuning up his double bass. Then she hauled herself out of the deck chair and stood facing me. Ted began to play, slowly. The clear deep notes burrowed their way into the floorboards.

"You've been very kind, Mr King. I'm sorry to have to let you down."

Ted played a three note riff, over and over. It sounded like a question that wasn't being answered. I turned on him.

"Leave it out, would you Ted?"

When I looked back, Joan was already on her way through the door. I stayed where I was, offered Ted a cigarette which he refused, then lit one myself.

"She was a good little singer. Her fiance wouldn't let her come. She's going to get married instead. But she was upset. I was being a comfort."

Ted didn't reply, he just let his fingers walk up and down the fretboard as the room filled with cigarette smoke and low resonant bass lines. I stalked around, making a count of how many light bulbs were missing. Eventually Ted said, "That's a pity. She had a nice voice, nice singing voice. Bit of a loss really."

"How do you mean? A bit of a loss?"

"I mean it's a bit of a loss. Unfortunate that she was upset."

"You think I upset her? Is that what you're saying? Because you're wrong if that's what you're saying. She was only a kid. I was trying to comfort her."

"Yes," Ted said, strumming discordantly, "so you said."

"There are plenty more bass players where you came from!" I shouted.

"Really?" Ted said, his eyes closed in rapture at the sound of his own playing.

❖

The lights stayed dim and the mirror ball was still rotating. Under its shimmering light Joan's face looked like an image from an old news reel.

"Excuse me," I said as I reached their table, thinking already that I should have let the whole thing lie. Her husband looked up at me before she did, not a hostile glance, just a calm disinterested one. I stood with my hands resting on the table and nobody took any notice of me. They were distracted by the rumpus that was going on at the bar. Frank was protesting that it wasn't his round because he'd been on the phone when the last drinks were bought and missed out.

"I bought you one anyway. It's not my fault if you didn't drink it."

He and Ron – trombone – were conducting their argument at a shout, blocking the way to the bar for everybody else. Somehow Melanie had a drink already. She and Ged were deep in conversation, letting their hands touch. Finally Frank got his wallet out and things settled down again.

"I do remember you, now I come to think. It's Joan Brownlow isn't it?"

She looked up at me and said, "Yes, I recognised *you* straight-away."

"Who could forget 'Harry King's Bold As Brass'?" I said, with a flourish of little dance steps which I was embarrassed by even as I was doing them. Joan's husband asked me if I'd like a drink. "I'll have half a mild if you're going. That's very kind of you."

I watched her husband pick his way through the tables and I sat on his chair, more perched on the edge really – so I wouldn't be thought presumptuous.

"Good dancer your husband," I said, staring after him.

"He's a new man since his hip replacement. He's never off the floor."

I looked at her and then we both laughed at what she'd said.

"You know what I mean," Joan gasped, dabbing at her eyes, "he's never off the dance floor."

There was a pause then we both cracked out laughing all over again. The other couple at the table looked on with awkward smiles. I calmed myself and asked, "What was that band your mum used to front?"

"The Victory V's."

"Did they keep going or what?"

"No, not really. My mum stopped doing it shortly after I got married. She opened a fish shop on London Road."

"Oh." I let a chuckle slip through again.

"Only it never really took off like she hoped."

"No." I said, not knowing what to say. I could see into the darker corners of the hall from here. Rows of empty tables stretched back to the green exit signs. From the stage, if you screwed your eyes up, you could imagine the place was full.

Joan nodded her head and tapped her foot as though the music was still playing.

"And what about you Joan? Do you still sing?"

"No, no. Not for a long while."

"I find that hard to believe."

"I used to do the Talent Contests up to a few years back. But I became an asthmatic."

She said this as though it was a religion rather than a medical condition.

"I can't tempt you up on stage then?"

She shook her head and turned a beer mat over in her hand. Her eyes swept round the room, taking in the ramshackle stage, the squabbling crush at the bar, the pock-marked wooden dance floor and, finally, me. Too much Brylcreem again, my white shirt swelling over my waistband like leavened dough.

Joan's husband returned with the drinks and stood behind her. He rested his hands on the back of the chair while making conversation with the other couple who looked relieved that he was back.

"You were upset that day you had to jack it in, weren't you?" I whispered. "When you couldn't come on the cruise. Did you get over it all right?"

Joan straightened up in her chair and took a sip of Babycham.

"I suppose I must have. I'm still here forty years later aren't I?"

She gave a big laugh which degenerated into a wheeze. She pulled an inhaler from her purse and took two long gasps. I tipped some beer into my mouth. I drank off more than I intended but I wanted to get away. As I banged my glass down on the table Ted walked by and I grabbed him by the sleeve.

"Ted," I said, "Ted. Do you know who this is?"

Ted and Joan looked at each other and for a moment they resembled two different species who had been accidentally placed in the same cage. Then Ted readjusted his mask, scratched his head and put on a funny voice.

"Give me a clue Harry, for God's sake!"

Joan laughed, as did her husband and the other couple. Ted has a way of including people with his cheap tricks which I can't figure out.

"We better get back. The natives are getting restless." Ted said, wiggling his eyebrows up and down and getting another big laugh. Then he took me by the arm and led me towards the stage as though I needed directing.

"It was Joan Brownlow," I said, "do you know we auditioned her nearly forty years ago?"

"Did we? Both of us?"

"What do you mean?"

"She doesn't look like she'd have had it in her."

Ted laughed and displayed a row of crooked teeth. Then he put his arms round my shoulders and breathed all over me. "Between you and me Harry, it's a bit like holidays isn't it? You know you've been there, but you can't remember what year it was or," he paused and looked both ways as though he was crossing a busy road, "or if you brought back a souvenir of your stay!"

He threw back his head and laughed.

"You're sacked Ted," I said, just came out with it like that. He smiled and looked into my eyes. He was still smiling when he said, "You what? You can't sack me."

"You're out of the band. As of this evening."

"No, I mean you can't sack me. When it comes to it you can't go through with it."

"I'm getting rid. You've overstepped the mark."

"You stupid old get. How many have you had?"

"You upset that young girl."

"What young girl?" -

"You're a bad moral influence."

Despite my sternness he continued to laugh. He took hold of

me and waltzed me round the floor. I could see people's smiles flashing by.

"Harry, you're not being fair."

"Life isn't fair, Ted."

"That's true, I mean," a little pause here while he built up to the killing joke, "Glenn Miller died in the war and you survived. What's fair about that?"

Ted was still shaking his head as he picked up his double bass and prepared for the next number. He began shouting over to the other boys and some of them applauded.

We re-started with a waltz, 'Who's Taking You Home Tonight?' with an arrangement nicked from Joe Loss. It had a trombone intro which kept Ron happy despite the fact that his teeth were still missing. Once we'd got all the dancers back on the floor we did a quickstep version of 'All My Loving' and I was thinking how Joan Brownlow had been such a small girl. She was still the same now. A bit of extra weight on her hips and a few more veins on her legs but she'd probably had kids. I'd forgotten to ask her. I went on about that bloody audition instead as though it mattered after all these years.

After the Beatles number the programme was to go into a calypso called 'London Is The Place For Me'. I don't know why we keep it in the set. It's a dog of a song and Latin Americans only go down well at dance exhibitions. Before I announced it I reached for another tablet then realised I'd already taken them all. My heartbeat was coming in rapid little bursts.

"We'll do 'Maybe This Time'," I said to the band. There was a disgruntled rustling of music sheets and I heard Ted say, "Now I know he's lost his marbles."

After a few bars I realised it was a mistake. It's a bit drab without a vocalist, just that plodding verse and hysterical chorus.

And there was nothing much for Melanie to do until the end and even then she had to use the brushes. You can't even waltz to it properly because it's four beats to the bar. I half turned towards Joan's empty table and I knew that I'd chosen it because I imagined she would get up and sing. She'd be a bit croaky at first, but then by the second verse she'd really start to belt it out. Her voice would fill the hall and the band would be surprised and impressed. Her husband would look over and he'd be smiling and tapping his foot and at the end there would be an explosion of applause.

Instead of which, the brass section were swaying from side to side in mock unison and Ted was missing every other note altogether and talking at the top of his voice to Melanie. And she was giggling with her head down and her shoulders shaking. And Ged. . . Jesus, Ged was playing a different tune altogether.

I looked towards the door and saw Joan's husband helping her into her coat. He was a kind looking man with thinning curly hair, dressed in a grey suit and immaculate black shoes which he wore just for dancing.

FLIGHT
Glyn Brown

✢

✢

1962: Five

A first – the first? – memory of her, or the first that seems to count: dancing in a rainstorm in a navy and white polka dot dress. There is a cigarette between her teeth, which in your dreams will become a rose, there is a light like a lightning strike in her eyes, and her full skirt swings up around her knees as she holds it tight in her fists.

The Bowes Park Road isn't used to this. Car drivers honk and wave, or begin to swerve, and pull out of it just in time. Lorries slow down as they pass, prolonging their splashing of the four of you – the woman, and you, and Bridget Wilson, and plastic Jezebel (you call all your dolls Jezebel, for the hell of it and to watch the eyes of surprised enquirers). Bridget, fastened white-knuckled to the handlebar of Jezebel's pram, stares hotly in another direction. But you, summer dress plastered to your back and dripping between your legs, are mesmerised. Singing a rickety can-can, small hat lurching over an eyebrow, the dancing dervish takes your fingers and you splash together past the gasworks, giggling, because there's still so far to go before you're home, and because, before she started dancing, you were thinking of crying. The rain is warm, as summer rain is; it slides between her fingers where they clasp yours, and when she bends to stroke her face along your cheek, you see the drops, like tiny mirrors, or beads of sweat, on her lips.

The next day, Bridget Wilson withdraws the marble she gave you, her cut-out Bunty doll, and her friendship. "Your mother is mad." She says it in the playground. Look at your thumb, which has blue ink on it, turn on your heel, and begin to walk away.

"And she's a criminal! She ignored that sign, Keep Off The Grass. She ignored it."

You know better. Just keep walking.

1982: Twenty-five

On local rags in Croydon, Cromer and Cranleigh, you have conjured phrases out of nowhere to make the local news both engaging and entertaining, a pyrotechnic display of fun and philosophy. For five years you have done this. On nights of celebration – the local football team does well, the mayor's daughter marries brilliantly, a mother safely delivers quads – you have written like the wind, clattering on souped-up Olympias, a pencil, for good luck, stuck behind your ear. On days of tragedy – the team relegated, Sainsbury's razed by arsonists, horrific deaths in motorway pile-ups whose reporting leaves you shaking, drained and angry – you have struggled long over the right nuance. And, on days of no news whatsoever, you have made it up.

It turns out to be worth it. Your first job in Fleet Street, and in the features and not the news room. You write fillers, as yet, and do research. You are ecstatic.

After your first night, a long one, cross the scrubby hinterland of a darkened Fleet Street, where tumbleweed blows in bales toward Cambridge Circus, and enter a wine bar in which a woman has never before set foot, or not as a customer. Clear your throat in the sudden silence, but doggedly refuse to leave until you have been served.

•

1963: Six

Against the odds, you are a precocious reader. Teachers, finding the talent in you, sow you with words and watch them take seed and sprout. Encouraged, begin to scrawl laborious stories in blunt pencil on wide feint pages, but show them carefully to no one.

Home alone one cold afternoon, and searching for more words to consume, invade the clammy sanctum of your parents' bedroom and, beyond holding back, haul out the secret cardboard box which contains every theatre programme, every Christmas card and birthday card and telegram your family have given, bought or received. On Your Engagement. U2R1. Dear little baby, bundle of joy, pink. . .

One huge, stricken Valentine, the heart a pumping bludgeon of slick, red satin. Inside, like a tot's hieroglyphics, it says: To ym dalling hubsand.

Mirror writing. The writing of confusion. Puzzle hard, to check if that's the way the words are really spelled.

•

1983: Twenty-six

Knowledge becomes your friend, the dictionary your bible. Get distracted during office research by intriguing words, and disappear on their trail, wasting serious womanhours. Begin to take a perverse pride in using esoteric phrases understood by few, although these are generally removed from your copy by sub-editors who have had it all before, in different ways, but all, ultimately, as exhausting.

Find yourself elected to the paper's quiz team, and week after week defeat your rivals, hacks from Marxist broadsheets and right-wing old guard institutions, at game shows set up in dingy pubs where the floor is muddy with beer and sawdust (imported). Understand, eventually, that the team you're on is winning because you swot. You're keeping them at the top of the league table. Pride yourself on this, and pity their threadbare brains.

Read all the way to work, and all the way back. Browse bookshops in your lunch hour, grazing through Socrates and Simenon, Aeschylus and Atwood with ruminative application. Slouching down Charing Cross Road one lunchtime, head buried in *The Female Eunuch,* walk into a man with such a shock of red hair, you really should have seen him coming. For brief moments, both stand rooted to the spot, peering over the pages at one another. Decide you like the eyes, at any rate.

His name is Len. He thinks you need to refocus, perhaps on something further from your eyes than ten inches. He takes you for coffee. He has never read Germaine Greer or, come to that, much of anything. Fight, but go under. Partially.

•

1964: Seven

Win the class prize for Effort, not as flattering as the one for Achievement, but you still get a book token. Hopscotch home, your shoebag hanging from your shoulder and nuzzling the backs of your knees. Pull up short at your front door; everyone can hear what's going on within. "Bitch!" "Bastard!" "Moron! Thick-headed, brainless moron." The words they know: a small and, at times like these, a dwindling vocabulary. Aware that your slide has worked loose, drag it savagely through the tress it holds, tearing out many hairs, and stare at the three white ducks smiling foolishly on a blue bar. Inside the house, a table resounds. "Try to write letters, damn you. You *stupid* cow. Don't telephone everyone. How am I going to pay *this?*" There is the dull noise of something coming apart.

Hurl yourself inside, your mother's Sir Galahad. She'll need you now – she has no defence. What can she say? One thing she can't do, after all, is write letters, or not without endless effort. For you, words float and sing, plump and bright as schmaltzy Disney birds. For her, they're caterpillars that squirm defiantly on the page, then sprout wings and fly out of reach, misshapen butterflies that stick on her lips and tangle in her hair. Understand that there is no order in the world's chaos, and no way to begin to make it, unless you can name events and pin them down at intervals, preferably skewered onto paper by pen nibs, like tethering a flapping tent with pegs.

✣

1984: Twenty-seven

Move in with Len. Wonder if this is entirely the best plan, since he expects nothing of you and is impressed by your slightest achievement. But know you can't resist; after all, he expects nothing and is impressed. . . He is tender, too. The fly, the spider – probably the house dust mite, although he is allergic – are his friends. He will soothe your corrugated brow.

At work, vacancies open up above you on the newspaper. Pulling on seven league boots, begin to step into them.

1965: Eight

Tiny sobs, quiet now, bursting softly against her fist like dissolving doves. Get out of bed and, moving on muffled toes, bring her a cold flannel to lie against her hot cheek; it drips too much, leaking off her chin, your elbow, and she almost giggles. Why is she so silly? Why is she such a silly thing? Even an inexperienced, careless big sister wouldn't be laughing now. Sensing your stern concern and with, in any case, her heart not in it, she sobers, murmurs reassuringly, in the back of her throat, and stills. Ssh.

Hitch up your pyjamas at the knees, the way you have seen men do, and kneel between her legs where she sits on their double bed. Billow of warmth. Reach up the flannel because there is mascara, wet dustings like uncertain shadows, stuck around her eyes. Dab fumblingly until she pulls a face, pushing her nose sideways with a thumb and going, for two minutes, cross-eyed,

Harpo Marx right here for you.

Dab again. Annoyed at your clumsy work, wring the wet towelling into a pot plant, stubby, eight-year-old fingers bumping together like badly-rehearsed dancers. Whisper, Leave him. But you don't think she hears. She has turned and is looking, calmly, at her face in the moonlit mirror. She's watching her jaw swell. "My head aches," is all she'll tell you. Her head is always aching.

Say, Run away with me. The two of us. I can look after you. Feel wild with the thrill of it, desperate for the taste of it, the crazy freedom of the dark that's outside. Take her finger, the middle one. Begin to walk to the bedroom door, pulling at her hand. Let me take you. C'mon, let's go.

From the sitting room, just a door away, the wave of an audience's laughter surges to break against the orange-flock walls. "Take the money or open the box? What's it to be? What should he do, ladies and gentlemen? We can't hear you. . . "

Four feet from the screen, he's sitting like the picture you once saw of Abraham Lincoln. Hands rock-like on the crimplene arms. Feet jutting out in his slippers, tug boats ready to steer. A faraway, indistinct look in his eyes.

When he feels you there, a diminutive and reproachful figure, he says, without turning, "Just keep her out of my way, and keep her quiet." He sighs like a giant; look down at his huge feet. There is a weight of responsibility on you, and you don't know if it can stop you growing.

✣

1985: Twenty-eight

Split up with Len. Again. Finally, you tell yourself. "Why?" he asks. "What?"

Hurl about the room, fisting the air. "I don't know. I don't know. It's just how it has to be."

He strides to your side, holds your arms, which still try to flap like jerky chicken wings, and looks at you hard. "What have I done?"

But there is nothing. He fixes things around the place – broken fridges, flapping blinds, the dinner, a drink when you need it. He talks, on subjects you want to discuss, and listens to your responses. He caresses you in the night, his hands planing like seals down the funnels of your back.

His behaviour is beyond reproach. But he doesn't understand your passion, the lust for words, doesn't quite appreciate what you do. Begin to pack your things – photographs, books, a clockwork monkey, your postcard of the Chrysler building, typewriter, the kitten. You will all depart together, maybe tomorrow, maybe the day after.

And you do. Leave the flat, and walk into indeterminate space. Search for somewhere to pitch your flag.

✣

1966: Nine

Finish mapping out the tributaries of the Hudson River. Blow the last shreds of rubbing-out from your diagram, critically squint at it, then pack away your day-glo felt tip pens, biros and ruler in your Arsenal Forever pencil case. Behind you, the TV laps at the curtains, at the carpet. All that's visible of him, when you glance back from the kitchen table, is a massive, furry arm – like an orang-utang, from Borneo or Sumatra – resting a bottle of Barley Wine on the carpet. The *Star Trek* theme reaches a crescendo, luring you. Intend to watch it but, on the way to dump your books in your room, pass theirs, where the baby has her cot. On the bed, singing May to sleep, your mother. 'The White Cliffs Of Dover'. 'It's A Long, Long Way to Tipperary'. 'Pack Up Your Troubles'. Songs from a dislocated childhood, from a war zone and war years, your father's and your grand-father's time; songs to solace troops, soothing a baby to sleep.

Your mother sang these strange lullabies to her own little sis-ter – aunt Laura, who could do the splits and walk on her hands and wanted so badly to run off and join the circus. She sang them most often when they both were lonely in their isolated, evacuee years. A Cornish farm, lost in rolling greenery, where mum fed the pigs and milked the cows and no one noticed she still wasn't reading or that, when she tried to write, words came out backwards.

But now is now. Creep up on the bed, snuggle into a ball be-hind the warm shape, and listen to her back resonate with the songs. When May is asleep, get carried, a floppy, limby puppy, to your own room. "Let's see – a silver one-piece, your gran made aunt Laura, to wear in the children's gymnastic displays," she answers your drowsy question. "She looked like a beautiful fish." Warm hand, rubbing your calf. Stretch your foot. She holds it. "I think your sister has the same shaped back, Ramona. I think your sister will be double-jointed."

Try to touch your nose with your tongue. Say, "What about me?"

"I don't think so, poppet." She kisses your mouth goodnight.

"Just one set of joints for you. But that doesn't mean you have to keep your feet on the ground."

Close your eyes. Float, and dream, and fly.

✛

1986: Twenty-nine

Begin to hang around learned men, or men who have the woodenness, captivating egotism and touch of the aloof the learned cultivate. Their pristine other-worldliness fascinates you. At a party in a gallery, backing out of a press-starved artist's clutches, bump into a coat whose tweed is the deep, shadowy blue of Scottish gloamings. Its occupant turns, regarding you with cocked eyebrow and questing grin. Both stare at his coat, which is soaking up your spilt wine like a glutton.

"Please," he pre-empts your apology. "A pleasure to have some light relief in this crypt." His tone gives you Cary Grant, his expression is stage-woeful and, framing a face with this much youth left in it, the shameless streaks of grey at his temples look like go-faster stripes. He smiles at you more broadly. "Or perhaps it's not such a crypt. But, if you intend to stay a while longer – and I hope you do – " twinkle, twinkle go his eyes, "you'll need some alcohol back in that glass. May I?"

Theodore, you will learn – from him and from people you later ask in uncharacteristically giggly late night phone conversations – "has a reputation". He is a Writing Fellow at one of the lesser-known redbrick universities, a place which, during the obstreperous Seventies, kicked up quite a rumpus, and which has consequently slipped, on the university top ten, to a position of faded indignity. You are not to know this last; your encounter with higher education has been brief. "I went to Sussex."

"To do what?" Dexterously, his tongue locates and removes a shred of red pepper from an incisor. Notice a small white hair curling from his left ear, and find it unaccountably charming.

"To research a feature on their experimental rabbit breeding." Maintain a deeply studious expression, and twirl your glass reflectively. "Unforeseen developments had occurred. Project too successful. Lots and lots of rabbits. Careless, overworked lab assistant – mass outbreak. Guerilla bunny colony rings the place. Dawn raids on the campus allotments. Decimated carrot crop. Boy almost breaks his neck tripping over a rabbit on the playing field. Interesting feature. Need I go on?"

Theodore – who claims to be a novelist and poet – loves it, and finds you refreshing, he says, magnetic. It's mutual. He holds you rapt with talk of narrative structure, reality base, plot and counter-plot, Derrida, Levi-Strauss and Woody Allen.

"I could talk to you all night," he murmurs. But little talking is done back at your flat.

✣

1967: Ten

In March, see *Lady And The Tramp* and every single episode of The Monkees. Fall in love with Davy Jones, but think about him often as a cartoon character, a scruffy dog yodelling to you across the rooftops. Spend three weeks' pocket money on a framed, tinted picture of the singer in Woolworth's, where the saleslady tells you she's his aunt, and you believe her.

This is the year you're into photography, anyway. When the

funfair comes in June, snap away at everything with your new Kodak Instamatic. When you get the film back, the picture that stands out for sheer composition, the one you look at again and again, is one of your parents, lost in a kiss on the Ferris Wheel.

August. Floating laboriously, watch her from the sea as she paddles and laughs at the greedy foam's edge. Voluptuous, full as a fruit, in a pink and white candy-striped swimsuit, she seems as beautiful and as giddy as Marilyn Monroe. Not far from you, May gurgles and precociously vaults through the sea like a dolphin while, out where it's deep, he surfaces, spluttering, waves to the rosy woman, then plunges again, blue-black hair slick and shiny as an electric eel.

At the school open evening, her hair is like Snow White's, very long, very black, and her cheeks glow. People's fathers come across to talk to her, smiling into her eyes, until people's mothers pull them away ("Why is that woman *alone?*"). You and she stand, paired together in the middle of the room, like Bambi and Thumper on the ice, hesitant to step out. Drag her to your desk; it's like hauling a shopping trolley, okay once you get the momentum going. Sit her in your spindly chair and spread your paintings before her. She begins very slowly to turn the big, cracking and encrusted sheets, scrutinising every daub to its triumphant finale. Halfway through, she beams, and hugs you tight. And then her gaze goes on to take in something past you, over your shoulder, and she smiles. Turn to see your father who, still grainy with cement powder, sheepishly slaps at the dusty leg of his mildewed suit, then strolls across from the doorway and puts his hands gently on her shoulders.

"Ah. Mr and Mrs Price? We meet at last." Mr Dawson grins at you, shepherds them toward his desk – "Oh, leave the paint fiend where she is." Pull out your jotter and scribble in it. After five minutes, glance across. He's showing them your stories (you trust him), and she's smiling, and looking at his finger as it points to interesting words, measuring from what he says the way she should organise her expression. No one would guess.

✛

1987: Thirty

Theodore is an ungraspable lover, navigating the tangling reeds of commitment with the ease of a man greased for a cross-channel swim. He is evasive about his romantic history; perhaps a sunken galleon lies on the ocean floor, shifting painfully when the current eddies. In any case, your careers come first and, when you ask, he says he loves you. "Of course I do, Ramona," he murmurs, stirring his cappucino and considering the shapes of trees through the window. "You know it, why must you ask? Try to put your mind on something higher, dear, something other than yourself. For example, look at how sere, how skeletal that elm has become. Isn't there a strange, post-structuralist romance, in a way, to. . ?"

Screw up your eyes, and try to see what he sees. Begin to doubt that it is in you. When Theodore discovered your new job – editing the women's section of a daily newspaper – his congratulations rattled hollowly, like peas in a bucket, and the scorn in his eyes was like a hail of poison-tipped quills. There is, of course, a shelf-life to novelty, but Theo, for all this, still keeps on coming round, drawn by your repartee and bedsocks. Say less and less about what you do and, at night, when he has been able to fit you in between the endless campus late nights, roll away from him after making love and admit silently to the dark that you resent him. And yet, his intelligence holds you in ghastly, ghostly thrall. It elevates him beyond his actions; it is his pillar of light.

One evening, drunk and fizzing with recklessness, gatecrash a literary party. Theodore is surprised to see you. He tells you the party is boring, a damp squib, that he's only here because he has to be, etcetera. "Lucky old you," he says. "You could leave right now."

In the ladies room, as you brush your hair before calling a cab, overhear a woman crying in a cubicle, into the arms of a friend. From the things that are sobbed, and moaned, and confided, discover that this is Theodore's wife, and that you are not his only liaison. "A reputation." Ah, so. Outside, squirt your fountain pen down Theodore's shirt, tell him his poetry stinks, and leave in tears.

Sink quickly, without bothering to clutch the couch grass on the bank. Convince yourself you are indeed, on many counts, rather slow. Slink away mentally to the hacks' graveyard and loiter there, amid the dried up Tipp-Ex bottles and the expanding armbands and the green peaked visors. In your free time, stare stupidly at space. Abandon books, and the places where they are sold. There is nothing friendly there, nothing trustworthy either. Words are bastards, after all.

Concerned, your sister calls, in the night from many distant cities. She has an innovative high-wire act with an international circus of some renown. She takes death-defying risks, but only after learning how, by physical manoeuvre, to outwit her leaps, to diffuse their menace. Her lover is Alice, gravity-defying partner in their tumbling show. Together, they swing and leap and, gleaming with confidence, fall and catch and soar. They have a net – it is the law – but, she proudly claims, they will never need it.

"So what should *I* do?"

She says it's experience that gives her such grip. Knowing how to handle it when you miss the bar, or the timing's off and no one's there for the catch. Some grisly things can happen, she says; but it's worth it for the feeling when it works: the know-how can facilitate some really quite breathtaking stunts. "Anything else, wise one?" you ask.

"Rosin."

✣

1968: Eleven

When they fight now, put on your record player and dance to Rolling Stones tracks, turned too loud.

Spend a lot of time dressed in her raincoat and his trilby, a piece of rolled-up card in your mouth. Call yourself Ingrid and think about disappearing, taking off to far distant places, Humphrey reading you his favourite poetry during the flight.

Coming in from your evening paper round, hear her voice from the bedroom. It is summer, and motes drift on spears of warm light which finger between the drawn curtains. Her head's bad again; she wants a cold flannel. Tell her she should see about getting glasses, then squat beside her, and take one hand, with its broken nails. Cold water from the cloth trickles into the forests of black at her temples, losing itself on her scalp. She wants you – you can barely hear – wants you to do something about his tea. He'll be home soon. His tea should be ready. "Bugger his tea," you tell her, but you get up and walk toward the kitchen anyway. She says something. What? Quietly: What did you say, ma?

"He works very hard, your dad. Now then."

Such tenderness.

✣

1988: Thirty-one

Theodore calls. It has been a long day, you are tired, not pre-pared, although the two of you say lately that you are friends. Si-lent with shock at the sound of his voice, listen to the liturgy of his recent achievements: the crown, the pinnacle being his new book, on the brink of publication just in time for Christmas. Be-fore you part, request the return of stories you wrote, things which he had begged to see, and then declined to mention. "By all means," he assures you evenly. "They were all rather senti-mental, anyway. Beneath you. I'm sure you can do better. Tell me," you hear him draw on a cigarette and let it out, "why are women so obsessed with their mothers?"

Realise, in horrified, exquisite pleasure, that although he has never been rumbled, Theodore is the stupidest person you know. Suddenly feel loosed, freed. In answer to his question, explain that you really can't say. Sign off. Cross the corridor to the paper's literary section, confess your secret desire to break into book reviewing and, browsing lazily through the batches on the desk, fish out Theodore's oeuvre and suggest, "Why don't I try out with this one?"

Feed your machine some paper. Make coffee. For the first time in a while, relish a job.

✣

1969: Twelve

When she dies, wilting in the shade of an unsuspected tumour – which you later imagine lurking like a spider behind her eyes – miss it, because you're on a hiking trip with the school. When you are brought home, and stand in her bedroom, condolence cards shuffle, like sad white sighs, like tourists, on the insides of the window ledges.

At the funeral, there is much whispering, it seems, when the three of you – he holds your hands, a child on each side – walk behind the coffin to the front pew. With the first hymn, he falters, sits suddenly when everyone else is standing, and begins to sob hard into his hand, then gently into your shoulder. Your brittle heart melts a little.

It's summer again. On the lawn outside the church, wreaths float like jazzy halos. Imagine her appearing, putting one on her head, and leading you over the grass in a waltz or a polka. "I loved her so much," he is whispering, kneeling before you, looking at you. "So much."

Stare away over his head. In the sun-soaked meadow that adjoins the cemetary, May, not understanding what's happening, and also understanding, somersaults in crazy circles, her face strawberry-scarlet. The sky is cloudless, but for a stubble of white in the distance, like straggling birds flying somewhere.

An aunt wants to speak to him. He says, "In a minute, love," and leads you to a wooden seat. He takes your hands, jiggles them about in an awkward way. "I'd say your mother had what she really wanted from life," he gets out, eventually. "In that way, she was one of the most intelligent people you'll ever know." Keep your expression blank. "Do you see?"

For your thirteenth birthday, three months later, he gives you a small party, which you don't want, but it happens, anyway. Refuse to come in from the garden when your friends arrive and then, when you do, watch his huge, clumsy hands shaking the jelly from its cat-shaped mould and say, "You've broken it. The ear's come off."

At Christmas, when you sing in the school production of Handel's 'Messiah', tell him parents aren't invited, a blatant lie.

In the school pool, practise holding your face underwater, listening to the way noise gets soft and blurry. Finally, learn to swim beneath the surface. Fin about slowly there, for long, lonely periods, eyes open and staring at everyone's legs, skinny white creepers with bruises.

1989: Thirty-two

Your review of Theodore's book, typed by fingers whose nails you paint a luscious, chip-resistant flame for the job, is one of the most incisive critiques you have written. It's a stormer. Dispense entirely with the protective safety-net you usually employ for journalism and, the bit again between your teeth, surge back into the job with renewed vigour. Your first full-page feature in some time, about a woman who runs a Pestalozzi school, appears in a highbrow journal, and receives a huge postbag. Len calls up, to congratulate you, and invites you for a celebratory meal.

"I thought you might hate me," you say, your voice trailing a question mark.

"Ah, no. You were off on a word chase, in love with something that wasn't me. After the Knowledge, like some insane cab-driver." It's his joke. But the tone's ironic. Least you deserve. Anyway, the meal is good.

Better than these things, your sister and her troupe of performing friends are in town. Beneath the big top's tarpaulin, in the criss-crossing beams, she drifts with Alice through enchanted plains of air; they seem to caress in flight. And, as you crane back to watch their dance in the sky, it comes to you at last that this is how your parents were. For them, everything was physical. It was all choreography, a wordless way they could react together. Something for only two people, a blazing kind of ardour of which you and May were a captive audience.

After the show, still half-dazed with the new thought, take your sister and her many sets of joints to a small but intimate bar. She looks good, you're happy to say, brown and muscular, quizzing the bar man good-naturedly on the sugar content of his soft drinks before spiking her Appletize with gin. In an alcove seat, underneath a stuffed bear's head, talk about typewriters and trapezes, and now and then. She has made the effort to see your father this week; his message to you is to try Pan Am, "obviously a more frequent service than British Rail".

"Oh, God." Hold your glass, with its dribbles of condensation, against your forehead.

"No, it's okay," she assures. She stirs her drink with a swizzle stick declaring that Waterloo is Southern Comfort country, then taps it on the side of her beaker. "He's fine, spends most of his time looking at snaps from the old days." She deepens her voice, rolls the phrase out with a midwestern twang. And she says something else, begins some wild yarn, only you don't hear it. You're busy watching scenes that reel through your mind, photographs that come to life, everything transposed into a Technicolor *West Side Story* scenario. Your mother's flailing skirts at a dance; your father serenading her once, in the evening garden (May giggling her head off under the covers); his voice, bellowing curses in the kitchen, your mother's hissed threats and her hand, cracking a slap across his cheek. Scenes flicker faster: Theodore's pale and effete digits contrasting with May and Alice, tender seraphs grappling for each other's fingers on a bed of empty space; and you, nails coloured red as roses, hurling and mixing words not just as instruments, but as objects of passion. That is where the real strength lies, and where it always did. That's what matters. Taking your toes off the ground, taking the leap and the risk, in a silver costume, with your blood pounding, and no net.

Leave the place when they start to lock up. The street seems somehow out of shape, things leaking, structureless, from their outlines into dazzling, anarchic positions, letters and phrases on advertising hoardings flirting with your mind. White neon shining from a wall looks like a modernist bouquet, looks, if you squint, like a cluster of balloons. Think about grabbing it, then wonder exactly how drunk you are.

Your thoughts colliding, reach the end of the road in silence, just as a sudden rainstorm starts. And, without further consideration, and because walking is for those without wings, and because she's smiling and it seems the only thing to do, take May's hand and waltz her across the empty street.

LOW LIFE: COOL
C. D. Clark

✛

✛

"I can't think of anything but getting even with that scumbag."
Lou's face was puffy with anger. Her lipstick has smeared so that
'Regency Red' was cracked and fissured around her lips. For
twenty minutes her lips never stopped moving. They were like
two live red animals. Her companion nodded now and then as if
to prompt the flow.

"Honest, Jacko, can't you say anything?" Lou pouted after
another twenty minutes of the same. "Give me some advice,
bugger you. I've got to get even. Why should he be allowed to
get away with it? Bastard capitalist. Bastard fucking screwing
capitalist."

"If he wasn't a capitalist, you wouldn't even have a job. So
what are you moaning on about?"

"Is that the sympathy I get?"

"I've been sitting here all morning giving you sympathy.
Thanks I get," Jacko mumbled into his scrag of beard. He
opened another lager, tossing the clip towards the metal bin. It
bounced off with a ping and fell to the brown cord carpet.

Jacko made a move, then stopped. It wasn't his pad. If Lou
wanted to live in a dump like this he wasn't going to help her
clean it up. Mucky bitch. His own place was spotless. He did the
lino every morning after he'd got himself up and had his break-

fast. It was all part of the ritual. Up. Into the ice-cold bathroom in his underpants and pyjama top. A quick wash with a flannel, a rub more like, then back into the room to hurry into a clean denim shirt – he had two and washed them alternate days so there was always one clean – then the sweater, grey, Army and Navy but without the leather patches. Pull on the 501's, socks still on of course on account he slept in them. In this climate. Well. Docs last of all. Then to see to the inner man. Kettle on. Toast propped on the bars of the gas fire. Careful there. Scrape off the inevitable black. Single smear of low-cholesterol. Kettle ready now. Herb tea. Mint for mornings. After that it was clearing up. Crumbs off the formica work surface. Knife wiped under the tap. Cup rinsed. Then the lino. It was grey, pearlised, like walking on clouds. There was no need for filth.

"You're not even listening."

"What?" He realised Louey had asked him a question. Bloody hell. He reran his thoughts. Blank. "Sorry, love. I've got a lot on my mind this mo'."

"Not more than I have. By, you can tell your friends when you've trouble." She pursed the scarlet mouth, making herself look ugly and petulant. Her head turned.

He felt contrite. "I know it's tough. but you can't leave just yet, you said. So what's the choice? Stay on."

"I wasn't talking about that. Time, Jacko, has passed. I was talking about what I was going to wear."

"What for?"

"You really haven't been listening, have you? I told you. After the episode with the car he had the gall to ask me out. Again."

"So?"

"This time I accepted."

He tried to see it from her point of view. "You'll probably have a very nice time."

Her eyes shot heavenwards. "You're a complete bozo." She leaned forward and said slowly as if speaking to a half-wit, "I accepted, because, dear Jacko, it's part of my revenge."

"But Lou," Jacko tried to match her manner, "you're playing into his hands. He'll just love waltzing in somewhere with you on his arm. Where's the revenge in that?"

"Flattery, dear Jacko, fruitless flattery." But she looked pleased.

"Where's he taking you?"

"Somewhere."

"But where?"

"How the hell should I know?"

"Didn't you ask?"

"I'm too cool to ask questions."

"Anybody would ask. It's normal."

"Am I normal? How boring!" She stretched thin white arms above her head and let her head fall back. He could see up her nostrils. She still looked marvellous. Smeared lipstick, petulance, nostrils, armpits revealed, shaven though they were.

"Am I normal?" she said again, dragging out the syllables.

"You're one of a kind." He said it throwaway but it didn't matter because she wasn't taking any notice of him. Her eyes were shut and it was presumably Borthwick she was looking at.

"Actually," she told him, "he's taking me for a bite to eat. Those were his words. A bite to eat."

"Could be a Wimpy."

"Better bloody not be!" Her good humour was restored now. She had forgiven Jacko for not paying attention in class. He watched her with a sardonic smile. She was so easily pleased. Even though she might say she hated her boss' guts she was as excited as a little girl being given a surprise outing. She'd forget all about revenge as soon as she stepped inside that car of his. Tomorrow it'd be, "Borthwick this" and "Borthwick that", as if he were some tin pot god. Revenge would be something she'd claim she'd never even heard of. Let alone thought of using.

"You're looking cynical."

"I'm looking forward."

She raised her eyebrows.

"To tomorrow morning."

She got up and put her coffee cup in the sink. "Get going, Jacko. I need time to work out what I'm gonna put on."

Although Louey's bedsit was only across the hall from his own, Jacko didn't see her go out and he didn't hear her come in. It was almost half past five on the Sunday afternoon as he dashed out to pick up a bottle of milk before the corner shop closed that he thought he heard music coming from behind her closed door.

Monday, then Tuesday passed. There was a tap on his door just after he came in from work on Wednesday evening.

"It's me." She stood in the shaft of light that spilled out from behind him onto the landing. The lipstick was orange this time. Flame glow. Shrieking satsumas. He grinned at the thought. She'd once worn one that tasted of maraschino cherry.

He opened the door without speaking as she came inside also without speaking. He put the kettle on.

"I'm just making myself some tea. Want some?"

She wandered over to the black cooking pot on the gas-ring. "You'll make somebody a proper little wife someday, Jacko. What is it?" She peered into the pot.

"Carbohydrate."

"No, I mean, what's it called?"

"Dumpling stew."

"Mmn." She let the lid drop back on.

He reached across and put it on properly with a gap so it didn't boil over and make a mess round the ring. "Want some? It's nearly ready."

"I thought you meant *tea* tea." She looked across at the kettle.

He concealed his feelings under a blank face. Once she'd said he looked like Buster Keaton. It was useful, sometimes, to remember that.

"Tea for the lady." He poured scalding water over two tea bags and settled on the edge of the one armchair. That way he looked as if his listening was only temporary and nor could she settle herself in it for a long session. He didn't want to know about Borthwick.

"Well. That was the week that was. It's over." To his consternation her face puckered and went red. The orange mouth screwed right up and then opened like a fish's gasping for ant's eggs. Moisture glistened in the fissures that suddenly appeared on each side of her nose. Automatically reaching for a Kleenex, he pushed a handful towards her; then she was grabbing at his wrist, crumpling his hand inside her own, hanging onto his arm, thrusting herself against him where he still sat on the arm of the chair.

"Steady, love, steady." He put an arm round her waist, feeling awkward as she pushed herself closer and it slid down over her bum. He moved it cautiously back to a safer place, then regretted the action as it seemed like a caress.

"You're the only real friend I've got. Do you know that?" she sniffed, patting at the tears still flowing down her cheeks. "I can tell you what a bastard he is because you understand. Everybody else would just say I told you so. They'd be right glad to see me this cut-up."

"They wouldn't, you know. None of them would." He'd never met 'them' – the mysterious figures who peopled her anecdotes about work, but he had to say something.

"That Fay would. She'd say, 'I warned you. You went into it with your eyes wide open.' Anyway," she seemed to brighten with a positive effort, dragging a veil over her sorrow, giving him one of her old glamour-girl smiles and running both hands up under her dark hair, piling it up momentarily on top of her head. "It's always good to see how the other half live. Do you know how much he spent on what he called a bite to eat? Go on, guess."

"Ten quid." He frowned, not sure he was keeping up with her.

"Ten? Go on, guess."

"Fifty-two?"

"One hundred and twenty-five pounds and eighty-five pence, excluding tip. How's that for a bite to eat?"

"I could live on that for a month."

"Me and all. I nearly said something, but after what happened I'm bloody glad I didn't."

"Why, what happened?"

She gave a long-suffering look, as if to say that this once she'd given the world a chance to show her how good it could be, but it'd gone on and tipped her into the muck anyway. Jacko remembered that look later. "He brought me back here. With a bottle of champagne. We drank that. Then he said he knew a place where he could get some more drink and what did I like? I said Drambuie, testing like. And half-an-hour later he's back with not one but two bottles of it. 'This is for now. And this,' he held it between his legs, right crude, 'this is for later'."

"You don't have to tell me all this, you know." Jacko got up and pretended to stir the broth. The dumplings were ready to eat. Just right. "I'm going to eat this. You're sure you don't want any?"

"When I'm in the middle of telling you about my broken heart? How mundane!" She was joking. He couldn't understand what the tears had been for.

"If you can't eat and talk, I can eat and listen."

"Come on, give us a little bowl of it then. It smells good."

He turned up the gas fire and they sat in front of it with a bowl each and a plate of brown bread between them.

"So what happened? Did you have a row?" He dutifully supplied the prompt.

She shook her head. "Next morning he went out and got the Sunday papers and some pikelets for breadfast and some real coffee and a little tin of caviare and a big carton of double cream from the deli. He was gone about ten minues and it must have cost him a tenner just like that. He stayed the whole day and that night we went to the pictures in the West End. Another twenty quid or so. Later we brought some bottles of wine and a take-away in. More than we could eat. All the time they were piling up these foil containers and I kept saying, 'That's enough, we'll never get through it.' But he just shrugged. 'There's always the bin – unless you have some starving friends!' I thought of you, but I knew he was joking."

"I was out Sunday," he lied, trying to retrieve the joy of eating perfect dumplings in front of a warm fire from the recess of hell into which she was plunging him.

"You are po-faced, Jacko," she paused. "It makes a change. I'm fed up of folks judging. It was a nice weekend. I've no complaints. He's really cool. He made me feel cool. I was somebody else, just for the weekend." She bit her lip. "You know who I'm quoting, don't you?"

He'd lost her again. "What?"

"Him. It's him. That's what he said but I didn't realise the significance at the time. 'I'm somebody else, just for the weekend.' You know what I'm saying, don't you? The bastard's married, isn't he?" Her eyes moistened again. "I felt such a fool when I found out. Bloody hell. I should've been able to tell. What a dingo! I used to be able to spot them a mile off. Anyway. It was a nice weekend. And it certainly cost him a packet."

Louey moved away shortly after that to share a flat with a girlfriend in Kensal Green and it was nearly a year later when they bumped into each other again. It was Sunday and he'd gone out for a paper and bar of chocolate, intending to watch televison later. He'd taken out a hire agreement soon after Lou left, but liked to regulate his viewing instead of letting it become a habit, buying himself little treats and making a bit of an occasion of it all. Now he felt a hand on his arm. A woman he'd just passed in the street, one he'd not even glanced at, had followed him into the shop and after he'd picked up his chocolate she'd caught up with him as he joined the end of the queue.

"Jacko? It is! Same old Jacko. Didn't you recognise me?" She passed a hand over her forehead as if to reveal her face more clearly.

The mouth was pale, that was the difference. It changed her whole look. She seemed smaller, too. He couldn't work it out. He told her so, laughing, delighted, despite everything, to see her once again.

"You were always my best friend, Jacko." Her eyes saddened. In fact, now he looked closer, they'd been sad all along. It was just the transient greeting that had brought that look of animation to her face.

He held her thin fingers between his own. "I can be again, you know. But you don't come round. You should do. There'd always be a welcome."

She gave him that lift of the mouth that told him she didn't believe him. "No, not even you Jacko. Not even you now."

Before he could ask her what she meant, she stood on tiptoe and gave him a small, dry kiss on the cheek, then turned and was gone. He saw her head bobbing behind the crowd at the cash till. He could leave his place in the queue or he could stay where he was. Before he could make up his mind she was out of the door and by the speed she was going he knew he'd never catch her.

He paid for his chocolate and went out and was back in his room within ten minutes. Television was just a pale blur that evening. He tried to imagine her knock on his door but he knew it wouldn't come because he couldn't summon up the sound even in his mind. It was another while before he heard what happened and it helped clear up the desolation in her voice when she'd told him, "Not even you."

Somebody in the house had seen her. It was the man on the ground floor she'd always called Denzil for some reason.

"I say, you used to be fairly friendly with that brunette on your floor, didn't you?" He'd just finished making a phone call at the pay-box on his level and lifted his head when Jacko came in through the door.

"Brunette?" Jacko frowned as if he knew a hundred dark-haired women.

"Cheery sort of wench. Bit common, know what I mean? But friendly, that's what makes it all the worse."

"What?" Jacko stopped pretending.

"Saw her yesterday in not very pleasant circumstances, that's the truth." He cleared his throat. "Had to get a clean bill of health for my insurance company. You know how sticky they are these days? Well, who should be coming in but her – what was her name?"

"Lou. You mean Lou. Coming in where?"

The man lowered his voice. "The clinic. They send everyone these days. No stigma. But even so."

"She was going in?"

"And coming out."

Jacko was about to turn away. What she was doing was no concern of his.

"Going in looking worried. Coming out in hysterics. Yelling. Completely off her rocker. Claimed they were taking her off the treatment when it was just beginning to work. Making a hell of a row. Of course, who can blame her? I'd feel the same way myself if I didn't have proof I was clear." He was at his door by now and fumbled in his waistcoat pocket for the latch key. When he drew it out he gave Jacko a quick look. "I knew you knew her. But I know you didn't know her well." He put the key in the latch. "The times, old chap. The times we live in."

Jacko made his way upstairs. He couldn't go to her. He'd no idea where she was. He could maybe contact the clinic. Pretend he'd known her better than he had, but that would be no good. They'd take extra care with her address, imagining he was bent on retribution. He thought of what she'd said about revenge. About being cool.

"I don't ask questions," she'd said when he'd asked her where Borthwick had been going to take her. "I'm too cool for that." Too cool. He wondered about Borthwick. The wife. Others. He wondered if it was because she'd been acting cool that weekend, being somebody else, too cool to say no, too cool to ask the right questions, that had led her into this?

He pulled on a knitted cardigan when he'd taken off his overcoat and pulled up an armchair. He was watching television a lot these days. The gas fire and the blue screen were sometimes the only light he bothered with.

She'd said she was going out with him that weekend for revenge. He hadn't thought much to that himself. He remembered her look when she'd told him Borthwick was married and later that lift of the lip when she'd clearly been thinking she'd given life a fair chance to treat her right and what had happened was her own fault for being so naive. He remembered that look again and again.

"I'm somebody else," she'd said. "Just for the weekend." And, "It cost him a packet."

Outside, traffic passed constantly beneath his window. People coming and people going. It would always be so. That was life, passing by outside. As it became dark he went on sitting in the chair, a hunched shape illuminated only by the twin glow of gas fire and television.

He could taste the maraschino cherries on his lips.

BLUE MOON
Suzanne Cleminshaw

✜

✜

I had my first Shirley Temple when I was twelve years old. A Shirley Temple is a cocktail adults make for children. It is a mixture of ginger ale, grenadine and maraschino cherries and it is disgustingly sweet, but I found it dazzlingly adult. I felt I had crossed some sort of threshold.

We were at my cousin Nancy's house in California. She was my father's cousin, the one who was married to one of the first men on the moon. We were in their living room, which was sunken and seemed vaguely aquatic. Someone had closed the shutters and the fading light that glimpsed its way through breathed like shark gills on the softly carpeted floor, and the lights from the passing cars outside appeared like shocks sent off from electric eels. My Aunt Tully was there. She was Nancy's mother. I always got a kick out of her. She drove various sports cars that she wrapped around various telephone poles from Santa Barbara to Mission Bay, but she always emerged from the wrecks unscathed, blinking in the lights of ambulances and police cars like a celebrity arriving at an opening.

I sat down next to Tully and clicked my glass with hers in an affected way. Ever since we visited Universal Studios and the Hearst Mansion I had been imagining CinemaScopes hiding in corners, capturing every languishing move I made.

"Hey baby, where'd ya get that kimona?" Tully spoke in a slurring Ava Gardner way – in fact there was something very Ava Gardnerish about her – maybe the way her elbows peeped out from her half-sleeved suit jackets, or the fact that she always wore toreador pants when she went out shopping.

"My mom bought it for me in Chinatown, baby."

"Hey, I'm no baby sister – Oh ho no, not me." Tully rustled irritably and drew wet circles on the coffee table with the condensed water from her drink.

Tully was obviously bent on getting drunk. The whole family got pretty embarrassed by this when it happened, but I always had a lot of fun with her. One night she taught me how to waltz, not that white-gloved, pimply-partnered waltz, but one where you felt as if you could hear imaginary people on the sidelines snapping their fingers and saying "Cool stuff!" over their martinis. Another night we played out an act of *Who's Afraid of Virginia Woolf?* I was Richard Burton. I loved playing the fall guy to Tully. I loved pretending I was disillusioned, even though at the time I didn't really know what disillusionment was.

However, that night Tully was self-absorbed so I moved over to the window and opened the shutters a little. Nancy and Lars' house was on a cliff overlooking some suburb. All the houses were boringly flat like a row of boxcars left in a field. Pools were scattered among them, squares and circles of green, blue, aqua – their colors like the differing colors of planets photographed from far away. I was really excited about finally meeting Lars. He was always appallingly absent (appalling, my mother's word) from family meetings, weddings, etc. I had seen pictures of him in my parents' wedding album. He was tall, with a crewcut, and looked scientific. His eyes didn't seem to be in focus, like he wasn't actually there, but rather thinking about what was going on in some large and dangerous and gleaming laboratory. We also had a photograph of Lars and Nancy from their honeymoon in Monte Carlo. It is a black and white photograph. CAPRI CLUB 1958 is written in white cursive letters at the bottom. Lars and Nancy are sitting at a large round table, looking tan and happy and innocent. Lars had recently graduated from West Point, Nancy from Vassar. They had an unreal, naive quality about them that I have only seen in pictures from the Fifties, like the image of Christ seen within the folds of a liturgical napkin or a holy statue shedding tears – you wondered, was this real?

I looked back over at Tully. She was watching an ant crawl across the coffee table, with feline intensity. "Wanna see God?" she asked it and then smashed it with a loud thud. Everyone in the room jumped, and Tully looked up over her glass and said "Hiya, Lars!"

Lars was standing on the stairs above the living room. He was wearing some kind of military uniform. The front of it was co-vered with medals of every shape and size. Some hung from striped ribbons around his neck. In some childhood dark wisdom I knew he had dressed up like this for my brother and I, and I felt embarassed for him and for us. For him, because he must have felt stupid and pompous, and for us because for God's sake we weren't two years old anymore. Even kids know when they are supposed to react on cue, though; it is one of the earliest things you learn when your first aunt pays a visit, so my brother and I simultaneously said, "Wow!"

My brother and I rode in Tully's car. I wasn't sure how we managed this one. My mother tried every possible way short of rudeness to squeeze us into Nancy and Lars' Lincoln, but luckily my brother stood firm on wanting to ride in a car whose doors swung upwards like wings, so my mother hugged us like it was our last goodbye and we were off to Lowry's for steak.

Tully buzzed along the winding streets at her usual pace. We were moving so fast it seemed as if the houses, streetlights, billboards were being flashed at us in a slide show. I started to feel sick from it and closed my eyes. I thought of Lars on the cover of one of the *Life* magazines in our basement. He is standing in his space suit with the moon reflected in the glass of his helmet. I suddenly realized he was already History itself: one of the memories in the dark, serene space where events have already occurred, where they are closed and finished and poised like wax figures in a museum, protected from the changing space of the present

When we arrived at Lowry's I was dizzy. It was a big place that sprawled like a huge hotel lobby. All the tables were big and round with swivelling club chairs grouped around them and potted palms stuck anyplace they would fit, giving off the jejune air of plastic even though they were real. Jejune was one of the words I filched from my mother's *Vogue* magazines. Jejune and soigné. They sounded like the long necks of models. I liked to collect words that had the gentle arch of a neck, an ankle. Onyx, alabaster, jasmine.

Miraculously, my parents and Nancy and Lars were already sitting at a table, humming in conversation with the rest of the room. Actually, my parents and Nancy were talking; Lars sat rigidly upright in his chair, playing with a fork. He had changed from his uniform into a dark suit which looked like another kind of uniform. I sat down and stole looks at him when I could. I thought of a carved wooden monkey my grandfather had got for me in Bali when I was five. I thought of it sitting on my dresser at home, its monkey hands clasped about its monkey feet. I had grown attached to that monkey because it was foreign and strange and because it had a smooth mahogany philosophy about its face. Lars possessed that same calm detachment about him, as if he rotated around his own axis, apart from this world.

Tully was sitting in between me and Lars. She was singing softly to herself, and I saw that she was stroking one of Lars' hands meditatively. She seemed to have a soothing effect on him, because he let go of the fork and leaned back in his chair.

"Where'd you get all those medals?" I asked politely. Politely, because what I really wanted to ask was "Were you scared? Does everything seem strange to you now? Do you feel strange?"

"Diplomats. Presidents. Kings." Lars smiled at me. "They all looked the same to me after a while."

I pictured them all marching up to him with their medals and medallions. I saw them marching like diplomats in black and white World War I newsreels with those strange tipping walrus steps.

"Did I ever tell you about the time my steak fell offa my plate onto the President of Bolivia's lap?" Tully asked in general and Lars was carried off onto another current of conversation.

While coffee was being served, Tully went off to another table to talk to a woman with piled-high hair and Lars looked over at me and smiled again. "Was it really strange being on the moon?" I asked him before I could stop myself. The band in the corner began to play, which gave my question the quality of a line from a bad movie.

Lars looked down at his coffee. "I don't know – it didn't seem real. It was kind of like being on a desert at night." He talked in a low, shy voice. He reminded me of my science teacher back home that I had a crush on. He was always fiddling with Bunsen burners and complex elements while kids threw frog intestines around behind his back. But I liked him because he seemed to know secrets and he was fearless. He would blow things up and cut things open with the bravado of a magician, priest, surgeon.

"Was it very dark?" I wasn't sure what else to ask. Lars looked over at the band and then at me. "Would you like to dance?" he asked.

I followed him over to the small dance floor. The band looked like a big bowl of fruit – they were wearing tropical coloured clothing, tangerine, yellow and green – and playing favorites from Herb Albert and the Tijuana Brass. Each swish of the drum brush felt like the citrus spray of some huge orange. I had read that children and adults have completely different sensory worlds, as different from each other as humans are to cats. I wondered how Lars heard the music.

Lars twirled me. I had danced with my father, uncles, brothers, Anthony Caccitoria my sixth grade boyfriend – but never with a real adult, an astronaut. I felt onyx, alabaster, jade, soigné.

Lars went into a standard box step and looked down at me. "It was dark. The moon. It made me realize why we are all so afraid of the dark. When you are up there and it is on all sides. Endless." He looked down at our feet moving together. "And it is not gentle; it is harsh. You feel as though there should be music of some sort – but it is completely silent." He looked up at me again. "I cannot explain it. It felt as though there should be something more." Lars suddenly seemed embarrassed.

"My science teacher said it weighs 81 quintillion tons."

"Yes. It is very solid." Lars smiled again. My science teacher also said that it moved over our heads at more than a thousand miles an hour and followed certain set laws. I just couldn't figure out the laws of the inanimate. Laws of nature seemed fairly plausible because at least there was living instinct flowing through veins – but what made rocks in space obey laws? What made them always travel in ellipses, faithfully moving onwards like a flock of dim-witted caravans, set on their course towards Hercules, the Earth like some Mexican New Year's caravan, lights bobbing, music blaring? The song ended. Lars led me off the dance floor.

"What did the Earth look like from up there?" I asked when we sat back down at the table.

"When we first saw it from the rocket, it just did not look real. I would say to myself, 'That is the planet Earth.' But most of the time I could not believe it." Tully came back and sat down between us. I was surprised that Lars continued to talk. "But then sometimes it would just strike me, that yes, that *is* Earth and I would feel just shattered." Lars glanced sideways at Tully and then leaned closer towards me. "Something else about it. It made me realize that we are always upside down." He leaned back in his chair. He picked up a fork and twirled it. "It sounds very silly. Of course everyone knows this. But it is quite an overwhelming feeling when you think about it all the time."

Shattered. I had never been shattered. Or devastated. It sounded so glamorous. Like Myrna Loy or Katherine Hepburn in movies where they have to decide between two different men and they are just completely shattered and have to have their maids bring up fresh gin and tonics and cigarettes to soothe their trembling hands.

Everyone was getting up to leave, and when we got past the heavy doors that looked like Hawaiian masks, the parking attendants already had the cars idling at the curb. We all got in our cars and as Tully tore out I could see my mother's pale and frightened face in the back window of the Lincoln.

Tully turned around in her seat to look at me. "Boy oh boy sister, I don't know how you got Lars to talk about that old moon trip of his. The only thing he'd ever tell me about it was that it smelled like gunpowder. Gunpowder! Can you imagine? I said, baby, you sure went on a hellava long drive up there for nothin' kiddo!"

I was only half listening to Tully. I was thinking about being upside down. The more I concentrated on it the more awful it seemed. To realize we are on some kind of freaky amusement park ride we can never get off of – the Earth like some huge breathing and pounding monster rolling and spinning and all of us holding on by some principle we can't even understand.

II

I was majoring in literature at a college in New York City and was supposed to meet Tully and Lars at the Plaza for lunch. Lars was in town for a few days. He was separated from Nancy and living in Indianapolis selling Lincolns. Tully and her husband Forest had a condo on 56th Street and she loved the Plaza because it was next to Bergdorf Goodman. Tully always wore suits made of the kind of fabric you only see in Bergdorf's, the kind that you thought had died on the pages of Forties fashion magazines, all dyed to the color of camels and salmon and parakeets.

The day Tully called to invite me, I went and looked Lars up in the sets of encyclopedias at the University library. He had become this enigmatic figure to me, one of those people in your memory who seem to dodge around a corner in the corridor of your mind every time you try to place them. He was in all the encyclopedias. I remembered when I was little I wanted to marry a prince, not for the jewels and the country homes and the hushed voices at your approach, but so that I would be in the World Book Encyclopedia. It wouldn't matter if boundaries changed on the veiny maps, I would forever remain the Queen of whatever kingdom I was Queen of and the dates of my birth and death would be printed year after year and distributed worldwide. But I noticed when I looked at Lars' entry, that the death date wasn't filled in, and I realized that this would be the only thing left to fill in – everything else in his life, of distinction, had been done, finished. A closed door.

I walked up Fifth Avenue from the Village wondering if I should cancel. I always felt trapped in the Plaza's tea room. It seemed like a huge rickety canary cage, surrounded on all sides by the big cat of New York. But then Tully always lifted my spirits and Lars seemed to offer the mystery that my life lacked at the moment.

I had recently had my first sexual experience with a literature major who read 'Ode To The West Wind' to me. This had made my knees tremble, but the experience afterwards was comparatively disappointing. Once we reached the bed he lost all his poetic glamour and turned immediately into one of the heavy breathing quarterbacks I had encountered in back seats in high school. I was starting to see what most people started to see once they went away to college. That there are two sides to life – the poetic and the real.

When I arrived, Tully and Lars were sitting at a table by the small orchestra. Lars stood up when I came to the table and shook my hand. He looked pretty much the same. Scientific, but with a suburban veneer on top. Like the businessman down the street who helps his son build *papier mâché* volcanoes in the basement and sets up chemistry sets from the local toy store in the garage. I thought about my crush on that sixth grade science teacher. I had thought he held mysteries, secrets. But actually he was on the other side of the fence.

Lars was much more talkative this time. He seemed relaxed with Tully and me. He talked about the car dealership, his house, his neighborhood. I pictured him in Indianapolis. I pictured him in his big Colonial replica house in the suburbs and I thought of that back door open, crickets chirping, that far away train, Midwest feeling you get out there. Maybe this was what he needed. Maybe it made him feel not so strange. Even though at that point in my life I spent a lot of my time disdaining suburbs, I also knew what treasures they held. The expectant sound of crickets and of slamming screen doors and the scratch of a record playing Brubeck in a hot upstairs bedroom. You can walk forever down a tree-lined street lit up from the lights of living rooms and the moist air propels you forward like a familiar sound. The suburbs give you moorings, make you feel that there is something more than gravity holding you down on your front lawn.

"I hear you are a literature major," Lars was saying to me, "I have been writing some poetry."

"Really? That's great. What kind of poetry?" This was making me nervous. Adults weren't supposed to write poetry. You didn't do that in the suburbs. None of my dad's bright green golf-slacked, Scotch drinking, grey-templed friends did. If you wanted to write poetry you didn't live in the suburbs.

"All sorts. Sometimes I try haikus. You can think of them while you are driving, or while you are cutting the lawn."

"That's wonderful. You'll have to send me some." I saw him at his car dealership in Indiana. I imagined him sitting in a flashy Town Car on the showroom floor, the new hot smell of it evaporating off the seats, jotting down haikus on the back of his sales cards, counting out the 5-7-5 syllables, the other salesmen whispering about him behind their glassed offices.

Lunch was over. Lars hailed a cab for us out in front of the hotel. He was going over to the zoo and Tully was coming to see my Village apartment. As Tully was giving her usual precise directions to the driver, Lars leaned through my window and handed me a slip of paper. "It's one of my poems," he said and then stood back and waved. I waited until we were out on Eighth Avenue before I unfolded it. There were only two lines. The agony in the Garden/The ennui of Sunday.

I crumpled the paper up before Tully could see what I was reading, and for a while my eyes couldn't focus on any one thing, like when you've done something really embarassing and your mind just races and you want to just duck out of the situation and run for a few miles until you sweat it all out.

"So how's this romeo poet you're seeing, sweetie?" Tully asked as she lit a cigarette.

"Oh. Same as the rest. Not as ethereal as I thought." I tried to laugh.

"Oh well. Everybody's after mystery, baby, and the saddest ones are those that have it explained to them. Facts ruin everything."

III

I was waiting in the Casablanca railway station for Lars to meet Tully and me. Lars was living there, and Tully and I were stopping for the afternoon to see him before we went on to Agadir and the sea. Tully was arguing with one of the porters about holding our luggage for a few hours. I was watching the row of clocks above the doors click out the time for London, Rome, Stockholm. On the train from Tangier, I heard a woman say to her husband, "Look at the hills." She said it in a slurry kind of way while she was nudging off her shoes, as if she had to mention them in the same obligatory way you buy a postcard for your boss, and the yellow hills that seemed before to unravel like lions' manes outside my window suddenly took on all the glamour of ash heaps. Now with each click of the clock I heard the same sighing statement. Look at the hills. Click. Look at the hills. Click.

"Sometimes I do not know why I travel in these countries. The religion of these people absolutely warps their minds. Hold this, will you, sweets?" Tully held out a compact to me and I held it open for her while she performed an extraordinary balancing act with lipstick, powder, eyeliner. "Have you noticed their eyes?" She looked up from the compact, horrified. "They are not human eyes – it makes me believe in reincarnation. They were once these cats and these cats were once them – one whole long and endless cycle." She waved her braceleted arm at all the cats roaming through the station. Most of them were black and dusty and missing ears, tails. They were sitting on the benches, on the ticket counters, one was even on top of the large handwritten timetable. They weren't like the cats at home, the fat ones that sit in windows and are disinterested in everything. These cats were watchful, they had dark eyes that contained some kind of perpetual movement behind the irises, like children hiding behind bushes.

Tully was irritable on this trip. We had decided to come to Morocco because Forest was having an affair and I was deciding whether or not to get married. I had seen Forest with his girlfriend one night by the fountains in front of Lincoln Center.

She looked dull compared to Tully. I couldn't help thinking of Tully's bedroom overlooking Fifth Avenue. It smelled of perfumes made by Givenchy and Chanel that are no longer manufactured, and there were glimpses of her animal-colored clothing on divans, peeping from wardrobes, slipping from drawers. Why did this all seem so alluring and soigné when a woman is twenty or thirty and then suddenly so helpless, hopeless after she turns fifty, sixty?

I had other things on my mind, though. I had graduated from college and was dating a man who was finishing law school. He had proposed to me a few weeks before Tully and I left for Morocco. I loved him, but then every time I thought of being married I had a picture of myself standing in the laundry room of a new house in Poughkeepsie on a rainy day. It gave me a Sunday-depressed feeling. It reminded me of being on one of the rides at Disneyland. You went on these little boats through a man-made stream inside a large amphitheatre. The boats glided by mechanical moving *papier mâché* figures that represented all the nationalities of the world – on your right were Eskimos ice-fishing and chewing on blubber, on your left were Mexicans making corn tortillas, then you turned a corner and headed straight on to Italians stomping grapes. Throughout the whole aquatic journey the ecstatic tinny tune of 'It's A Small World After All' was piped through enormous loudspeakers. In a little over seven minutes you had glided past the whole world and its peoples and customs. It took me the rest of the vacation to recover. Some people might find it a cheerful and uplifting thought that you can enclose the world within one hot and dusty amphitheatre, but I found it utterly disheartening. After you see the world, then what? Then where do you go?

Lars came into the station followed by his driver. The driver looked at me closely and then asked in very clipped syllables if he could carry anything for me. He did have the same eyes as the cats; Tully might have been right. But while she was annoyed by the resemblance, I found it enchanting. I followed him to the car and got in.

Lars looked older. When he smiled his bottom teeth showed more than his top teeth. Tully once told me this was the first signal to phone her plastic surgeon. I thought of all the millionaires that came to Morocco and lived debauched lives. I wondered what made him leave Indianapolis. It seems that people who live by illusions are either strengthened or destroyed by them. Maybe Morocco was strengthening to Lars, maybe it was the strangeness he needed, not normality. When you are in a room full of completely bizarre people, you feel yourself to be very normal, even if you are a little eccentric yourself.

We reached a restaurant on the beach. It seemed completely deserted. It was a big restaurant and when we entered I saw that there were only a few other couples dining there. Our footsteps echoed on the marble floors. There was a museum quietness about the place. We sat down. Lars had insisted upon the driver joining us – it was very hot outside – and he sat opposite me at the table. Tully seemed a little ruffled by this, but settled down once she got a drink and began to commiserate with Lars about failed marriages.

A heavy breeze rotated around the room, set off by large fans latched like huge brown insects to the ceiling. It was a humid breeze and made me think of the flapping pieces of wet rubber at car washes. I looked up from my water at the driver and his stare washed over me in the same sloppy mirage of heat. I thought of how I could follow him through the intricate passages of the Casbah, follow him through the low doorway of his house, past his mother and sisters washing olives in the courtyard, up the stairs and into his hot pink-painted bedroom with Rolling Stones pictures on the wall. I could live in that bedroom and buy chickens and rice for his mother in the market, and on full-mooned nights go to the beach with one of his mystical brothers who would tell me my fortune. I could become lost here too.

I had read somewhere about the vomeronasal sense. It is a mushroom-shaped disc at the roof of our mouths – some remnant from our past Mesozoic lizard lives – which can smell or sense sex and fear in others. Sex and fear were sitting at our table like a loud woman with too much perfume.

Lars asked me about my impending marriage and I asked him about daily life in Morocco. I wanted to ask him about his poem. I wanted to tell him I knew what he meant, that I couldn't get rid of that Sunday feeling lately, the feeling like you have stayed in all day and have read too much of something too deep and feel like life has not much else to offer. But it seemed as though I was looking at him through binoculars, and I wished I was twelve again, wearing a kimono and feeling dramatic and able to ask people questions that make them answer honestly.

I tried to think of all the questions I had bottled up in me that night in California, but I couldn't think of any of them. I had stopped worrying about why inanimate objects follow laws; I no longer had CinemaScopes trailing around behind me. There didn't seem to be any more exciting thresholds to cross.

After lunch we drove up in the hills to Lars' house. It was blue and white and stood among a grove of olive trees. There was the smell of mint in the air, and the afternoon chanting of the Koran rose from a small valley below. The chanting seemed to grumble beneath our feet, rise up through the rocks, run through the trees like an electrical current and cause a static twitching of their leaves. I remembered seeing a signpost in the Tennessee mountains that said, "JESUS IS COMING SOON". Soon. Sooner. Soonest. The air crackled with it. The house was dark inside. As we moved down the corridor towards the living room I could hear another voice chanting, although it wasn't the Koran. When we reached the living room I could tell it was coming from something hidden under a long blue silken drapery. I walked towards it. Lars came up beside me and removed the drapery. Beneath it was a large black raven with a bright yellow beak in a bamboo cage. "Biere, Schweppes, orange." The words came from the bird's beak, yet it seemed impossible – they rolled outwards and formed a whole landscape. Venders yell this on the beaches of the Riveria and the raven mimicked their cadence exactly. The 'R's' rolling like coins in a gutter, the end of Schweppes sputtering like a firecracker in wet grass and orange lascivious and curved as a woman's hip – all together the words sounded like a miscellany of objects tumbling down softly carpeted stairs.

"It reminds me of Monte Carlo," Lars said, looking at the raven.

"Of your honeymoon?" I asked before thinking of tact.

"No. Just that time."

There was a long silence and Tully started fumbling with her purse and the train timetable. Lars quickly showed us around the house. Most of it looked as though no one lived there. Everything was set perfectly in place – the ashtrays, the candlesticks, the vases – all seemed to be holding their breath as if in anticipation of some party and Lars moved as a ghost among them, an uneasy spirit making sure his physical belongings were not being disturbed by mortals.

Lars and his driver brought us back to the train station. Tully got our luggage from the porter and we somehow managed to get it all onto the overhead racks with Tully puffing her cigarette and saying that we should have taken a plane. We settled ourselves on the uncomfortable benches and Lars got off the train and stood on the platform. I busied myself with something in my handbag so I didn't have to look at him. I realized that I felt uncomfortable looking at him because it was like seeing myself in a mirror when I didn't expect it. Finally the train began to move, and I put down my things and looked out the window at him. Tully was opposite me, looking at her reflection in the window, rubbing lipstick off her teeth with a tissue. I could see Lars through the wavering image of her. He just stood there, his arms limp at his sides. He looked like he could be a statue, a statue in some noble and deteriorated garden. I wondered where he would end up next. I watched him as long as I could and just before the train turned the bend I stood up and stuck my head out the window and waved.

SCORCHED EARTH

Judith Condon

SCORCHED EARTH

At ten o'clock, feeling uneasy, I put aside my book and rake what's left of the coal to the front of the grate. Ash falls down and glows between the bars. I lift and lower the door-latch quietly, though there is no one to hear it but me. Out in the hall the cold is waiting. I feel it on my face and neck. I feel it rising through my slippers from the flagstones as I lift my coat from its peg. The sheepskin chills my shoulders at first, and my hands are already losing their warmth as I slip the buttons through the button holes. But I do it easily because the holes have stretched wide with the years.

The kitchen is warm enough. I stand for a moment at the window, looking out through the darkness. The farm cats are fighting again. Cold moonlight picks them out on the dry stone wall – the lean, buff-coloured tom and his young white rival. The white cat squeals, then drops into Hindley's field and out of sight.

I open the door of the Rayburn and shoot in some coal. It is foolish, perhaps, this keeping two fires alight. But I've no wish to huddle day and night in the kitchen. And the warmth will not be wasted. It will rise up the chimney breast and keep the night frost from my bedroom; it will warm the little pan of oatmeal I've already put to soak for my breakfast; and the coal laid on top of this coal tomorrow will in turn cook my dinner. Coal. What it meant to us once. So much it meant!

I push off my slippers, the right then the left, and slip my feet into my boots. The fur inside is warm from the stove. Perhaps tomorrow I will leave my coat in here too. I can surely find an old hook somewhere, to screw into the cupboard door. Just while this cold spell lasts. I open the back door and step down into the garage. I squeeze past the old Mini, pull my gloves from my pockets, and go out through the open doorway.

Outside the air is sharp and still. Its coldness scours the inside of my nose. I've been indoors all day – it's only now I feel fully awake. The moonlight shows me where to place my feet. Where there was soft mud a week ago, there is now frozen earth, moulded in peaks and ruts that send fear through my ankles. I make my way up to the gate, where frost is forming on the topmost bar. I lift and pull it open just enough to slip through, and hear the metal clang as it falls back into place. Out on the stony track I turn left and head up towards the edge of the moor. I am anxious not to fall. But my eyes are good. I depend on my eyes.

Only at the top, at the last gate, do I turn. Up here in the quiet I am rarely afraid.

A crescent moon, huge and tipped back like a rocking chair, is lighting the hillside. It catches the telegraph poles, the wires, and the roof of my house below. Hindley's farm, on the lower road, is hidden by the curve of the hill. Miles across the valley, beyond the wood, two or three clusters of light mark where other people are – the villages, the town. They seem as remote as the stars. And such stars! The sky as clear and dark as I've ever known it – but brimful of them. Does the sky look this way when night settles on the desert? I catch myself shivering. And suddenly – a classroom – a row of faces. And at the very front an under-sized brown-haired child struggling to recite from memory. I know her anxiety, my heart goes out to her.

"On Wenlock's Edge the wood's in trouble;
His forest fleece the Wrekin heaves;"

A ragged chorus of voices takes over:

"The gale, it plies the saplings double,
And thick on Severn snow the leaves."

My lips are moving, but no sound is coming from them. I am not alone, then, after all.

I can't get into the old chest of drawers. I've been out in the garage in search of a hook, but I can't open the drawers where the tools and nails are because the Mini is parked up tight against them on the far side. How long has it been like this? I simply don't remember when that car was last out. Back in the kitchen I've taken the odds-and-ends box from the dresser, and emptied it onto a newspaper on the table. There's the usual mess of items. I might even find a hook among them. But no. Here are the keys, at least, their worn leather tag. I step outside again. The driver's door is stiff and the seat seems lower down than ever. Sure enough, as I turn the key, I am reproached by a deathly rattle. I pull the choke out as far as it will go, and try again. Again that awful sound, and several times more. I think to release the hand brake and let the car roll back a few inches. I'm not even certain what's behind it. A miracle! Now that I try again, the engine groans into life.

And with the engine, Jim. No miracle, I hear him say. Good basic engineering. Always the same. Even propped on hospital pillows, when we knew he'd never drive again – still wanting to know how the old car was running. I could have replaced it, it wasn't the cost. Mad to have moved up here any way – didn't they all tell me so! – but an antique Mini? On these ruts and stones? Hasn't it always been my way to hold on to things too long?

It wouldn't have been my choice, this car. My right hand's not so stiff this morning and I spread my fingers against the glass of the sliding window. You always had to do that to stop it falling out when you shut the door. The glass is dirty. And now I can see him, leaning his hand on the bonnet. "Move with the times, that's the thing!" It was a Saturday morning he went to collect it. . . drove off in the old Ford Prefect, and just before dinner time we heard him calling, "Come and see!" There he is, leaning on the bonnet, shouting, never mind who hears him.

"Come out – come and see!"

"Look out the window, quick!" the boys are yelling. It might be a mirage and fade away. And we all have to get in, no arguments allowed. It's the big windows they like, the sense of space inside.

Cautiously I am pressing down the clutch and moving the gear lever forward. Like a learner driver, I am balancing my feet, listening for the right sound. Now it comes, a change of key. Unconsciously I lift the clutch and the car jumps up the slope. It shoots out through the doorway into bright sunlight – and stalls to a halt on the grass. Now I see just how filthy the windows are. I wipe the glass of the instrument panel with my handkerchief, and shade the dials with my hand. Seventy-four thousand miles. Seventy-four thousand miles up and down the county for the union and the party, for the good of the cause. And what do they all add up to, Jim?

✠

The hook is a great success. I have awarded myself a gold star for putting it up so well. I cleaned it with Brasso and I turned it with pliers til it was tight. Now I am sitting by the stove with a cup of coffee, reading from *The Oxford Book of Nineteenth Century Verse.* I am very pleased with myself. My coat is hanging on the cupboard door. Every day, whenever I want, I can put on my warm coat and my warm boots and walk up the lane. I am breaking the habits of a lifetime. I will not watch the news any more.

I am reading up on Alfred Edward Housman, "classical scholar and poet." I've split an enormous piece of coal with the poker, and heat is blazing out of the fireplace. The curtains are drawn against the dark outside. When I look up I see red firelight flickering through the soft yellow glow of my solitary lamp and the colours consorting along the bevelled glass doors of the book-case, one of which – the one with the key – stands a little open.

Housman, I read, was a repressed and controversial man, emotionally scarred by a failed homosexual love affair in his youth. He was clearly painfully shy. And fascinated by soldiers. I turn the pages steadily. Always the same pleasure in learning new things. I scan his savage prefaces to Juvenal and Manilius, and make a start on the Shropshire poems. I read of young men being hanged, or dying in battle. His style is meticulous. The mood is brooding and ferocious.

It seems that I. A. Richards, coming out of Housman's lecture 'The Name and Nature of Poetry' in 1933, is reputed to have said: "Housman has put the clock back thirty years!"

I dreamt in the night about Yuri Gagarin. Of all the things! Once round the world two hundred miles up in an hour and a half. I was there when he landed. It was so clear. He was stepping down from Vostok I – twenty-seven years old, so handsome, so proud. Why do I remember all this? His warm bright eyes, that gleaming row of fine white teeth? At my age too!

And here is his picture. Curiosity led me to take a stack of papers from the bottom of the old chest in the garage, and I have them spread on the kitchen table. There are all kinds of things, party publications, things we kept, well preserved in cardboard files. It's not the *Daily Worker* I'm looking at, but the *Daily Mirror*. The front page, April 13th, 1961. He has on a flying suit with a zip up the front – like those marvellous outfits little children wear nowadays. It fits snugly round his ears. "Today the *Mirror* celebrates the greatest story of OUR lifetime. . . the greatest story of OUR century. . . MAN IN SPACE." I am looking at a sweet smile, bowed lips with little curves at the ends. Boy in space, I am thinking. Babe in space.

What else is in here? Something I'd forgotten. July 13th, the same year. We were there, in London, visiting. Now those eyes under a wide-peaked military hat. Major Gagarin on his world tour lays a wreath at the Cenotaph. Underneath the caption, a brief report. We were allies against the Nazis, he said. The USSR paid with twenty million dead. The world would never forget.

We were believers then, in peace and progress.

I am turning the cuttings one by one. August. A high wall is built through the middle of Berlin.

✣

All day I've been grappling with history. Who would believe so much of life is wrapped up in the printed word! Having emptied the bottom drawer of the chest in the garage I simply couldn't stop. Mid-day came and went and I didn't feel hungry until now. I see we have been amateur archivists, believing we could learn from the past. Fabian pamphlets, *Tribune*, *The Daily Worker*, *The Daily Herald* – these by the score. Critiques of Korea, Cyprus, Suez, Aden. Proceedings of the Labour Women's League, minutes from the NUT. Mementos of delegations. Papers of the Anglo-Soviet Friendship Society. Articles by Orwell, Doris Lessing, Tony Crosland. Nye Bevan's 'In Place Of Fear', Strachey's 'Why You Should Be A Socialist.' I have stuffed pile upon pile into cardboard boxes and carrier bags and these are now stacked at the garage doorway. They put me in mind of an eviction, but without bailiffs, without spectators. The only other creature with any interest in the proceedings has been Hindley's white cat. He stood for a short while, not venturing in, but sniffing the air. I think he was hoping I might disturb a mouse.

I am tired and cold from my outdoor exertions. Some lentil soup, some cheese on toast will do me well. They are quick to prepare, comforting, and the kitchen smells good.

The fire is ablaze and I have some red wine warming on the hearth. I am waiting for a concert on the radio. My dear friend Leni looks out at me from within a small wooden frame propped under the lamp. Sipping my wine, I take it in my hand and turn it to the light. She is walking down Kingsway and I am beside her – both of us in summer dresses with padded shoulders and half-length sleeves. We smile at having our photograph taken. Leni, it's plain to see, is full of confidence. Her people are intellectuals. They are among the lucky ones, the ones who got out. Talking loudly, we turn into the coffee shop at the corner of Aldwych. Our companion, who is walking ahead, holds open the door. There is a table free by the window. He lays his camera on it, and we squeeze into the space. By the time our coffee arrives, Leni dominates the conversation.

"Opening this second front is Hitler's biggest mistake," she declares. "It will be hard. It will be very hard. But the Russian people, the Russian winter will defeat him. First his soldiers will be cold. Then they will be hungry. Like Napoleon. Think of Tchaikovsky's overture, the first slow movement. If they advance further, the Russians will retreat. This they know how to do well. They will dismantle their factories. They will burn their food crops. They will leave nothing for the invading army. Then the Nazi soldiers will start dreaming of home. Then they will know they are beaten."

The young man looks at her wistfully.

"And where will you go, Leni? When Hitler is finished, what will you do?"

"We will go back to Berlin. We will, how do you say it, spit on his grave."

Her face is animated. Her hands are talking too. We do not ask who she means by "we". We are happy to drink our coffee and listen.

"What a mess there will be. We shall need to rebuild a whole society."

"And what about you? Will you feel safe there?" the young man asks.

Leni answers without hesitating. "Who is ever safe? But Germany must never be a land without Jews. Our presence will be their reminder."

"Drink your coffee," I say to her, touching her arm. "Don't let it go cold."

I look into her face, her twenty year old eyes already dark with experience, and remember how much I loved her. Beautiful Leni, who believed in believing, who had the courage to go back.

I shut my eyes as the music takes hold – I have never heard Prokofiev played better. Now the cellos summon Nureyev to my mind. He is displaying, advancing into the ball. Eyes meet through masks, promises are made. Now it is Fonteyn alone, raising one arm against the moon. She moves before and through and after the notes – was ever a dancer so fluent? Now Mercutio is dead and Lady Montague cries revenge. This story is an old one. Ten o'clock approaches. I rake the ashes in the grate.

✣

Sometimes, lying in bed, I do not know whether I am awake or dreaming. The room is dark, I hear the clock ticking, and my thoughts go round and round. I am with Leni, in a restaurant. Something has prevented her from ever coming here before. The people opposite have paid their bill with a plastic card and I am trying to explain to Leni what it is. She has never used a cheque book, and my explanation is having to stretch to other matters. As I speak the table too appears slowly to be stretching between us, until Leni is so far away she can no longer hear me. Later I notice a square-faced man addressing a group of reporters. We are witnessing, he says, a new imperialism. Something is wrong. He is speaking the wrong language. I seem to remember him once before, his terrible school-boy French. But I am overcome with a sense of admiration for his courage. . . for his independence of mind. I try to say something but my own words seem obscure. I am offering a kind of toast I freely ignored that winter when all the lights went out, I am saying. I forgive you the police horse that crushed me against a wall. But as I raise my glass I see that it is misted over with my own breath; then the mist begins to break up, and a pattern slowly forms. I realise the pattern is made of men's faces. I look behind me and find ranks of men in helmets, standing in a field. Drawing near, I ask one of them to explain to me what is happening. We are miners, he says. We are Ukrainians. As he speaks he turns, taking off his helmet. I see that his face bears blue scars, made by the coal. Perhaps you gathered here to receive medals, I say. Are you not the flower of the working class? Do you not produce a third of all the coal in the USSR? We are on strike, he says, turning back and pointing at his companions. All of us. He puts on his helmet and is beginning to walk away. We have no soap. I cannot be sure that I have heard him correctly. Later I turn over. Now I hear an American voice. I see a figure striding down the hillside. I recognise him at once. You are Noam Chomsky, I say, walking towards him. I heard you speak long ago in the time of the war in Vietnam. It was not so long ago, he says. Have you forgotten? I have not forgotten, I reply. But there are so many things I find confusing now. Perhaps you can help me? Look over there he says, pointing to the hilltop. There is a new millenium not far away. America is staking its claim. Have you not noticed how strong Germany and Japan are growing? All at once his face dissolves and he is someone different. He is speaking in Latin yet

I recognise the words. *'Tis the old wind in the old anger* he begins to chant.

There is a thin white layer over the garden and field. The snow began early, but it has stopped now, and the afternoon is raw. It is important to keep moving. I put on my warm boots and my warm coat and walk out to where the Mini still stands at the edge of the field. There is a spare can of petrol in the boot, kept for emergencies. I take it out, leaving the boot open. One by one I carry the boxes piled inside the garage doorway, and stow them into the car. When the boot is full, I open the door on the passenger side and stack them on the back seat. History, scrawling lines across the map, chaining the future to the mistakes of the past. Fossilised time, spilling into the sea and burning beneath the earth's crust. You smoulder in nationalism, fester in religion. You infect the young and mock the old. What would my sons do with all this except sigh, and exchange embarrassed glances? I am piling my thoughts with the boxes and bags into the car.

Once again I walk to the gate. And again it clangs as it falls into place. In the white of the lane the only marks are the ones I have made trailing behind me as I climb. My steps fall into a rhythm:

> "The gale it plies the saplings double,
> It blows so hard, 'twill soon be gone."

I reach the top gate and turn:

> "Today the Roman and his trouble
> Are ashes under Uricon."

I am thinking of petrol, soaking into paper, and of a match

carefully posted through a sliding window. Perhaps the white cat will stand and watch with me. He will be barely visible against the snow.

A COLD WAR
Robert Cremins

A COLD WAR

It's happened: the snow on the road has turned to ice. Nothing can stop us. It's not long after dawn. As I put on my jumper Jay says rapidly:

– I'm going to the bathroom. Be right back.

– Sure thing, I reply.

It's a phrase I've picked up from him.

As soon as he leaves the room I walk over to his telescope, positioned by the alcove window. I look through the lens and focus in on the village below. I scan across to Dun Laoire; and from there to the city in the distance. Yesterday's fall – the first real snow in years – has frozen Dublin. The bad weather has trapped me here; as I prayed it would. Jay has seen much worse back home, of course; seen Colorado in December.

I scan back again. Bad weather, beautiful weather.

I hear the toilet flush. I compare the grey sea with the white land. I could do so all morning; if it were not for what's in store.

Though he is still in his stocking-feet, I can hear Jay's steps clearly.

– What are you doing, Muiris?

My eyelash flutters against the rim of the lens.

– C'mon, man, he adds. We've no time to waste.

– Sure, I say, turning and smiling. Let's go.

Jay is not looking in my direction. He's pulling on a pair of waterproofs. I'm going to have to survive without them.

– Let's do it, he says, marching toward the door.

I look back at the telescope. I've left it pointing out to sea. Whenever I come to Jay's house I find its front dipped low. He says he uses it to check out the neighbourhood.

I hear him drumming down the stairs. He doesn't have to fear waking his family. We've heard his sisters moving about already. And Mr. and Mrs. Sherman never sleep.

One more look around. Yes – this top floor is a great place for observation. Jay's floor. The bridge, as he and his father call it.

The footfalls stop.

– Muiris!

And resume.

I turn and trot through the door. Reaching the top step of the stairs I put my hand on the banister and pause.

Tobogganing.

I brace myself and descend. I run down with my hand gliding over smooth mahogany. I can feel my heart beating faster.

In the hall Jay is lacing up his boots – his paratroop boots. 82nd Airborne style, as he has told me many times.

– What kept ya? he says, grinning.

I smile and shrug my shoulders. I've always found it hard to answer his questions.

He laces the boots tightly: the leather creaks.

I dream about them. Sometimes I'm wearing the boots, at others a pursuer is.

I put on my outdoor shoes; the careful choice of my mother.

Jay takes a denim jacket off the stand and puts it on. I do the same with my duffle-coat. He looks at me, smiles and shakes his head. I don't blame him. It's true: this duffle-coat looks stupid on me – I'm nearly thirteen.

Jay reaches for his combat jacket. He puts it on over the other. I stare at the insignia. Odd shapes. But I know what they stand for. He has taught me all about this jacket. I know its history. Captain Sherman's jacket. Sometimes Jay lets me try it on. It looks better on him.

He looks like a man.

Jay is older. Only three months – but older. I'm not allowed to forget it.

We grab scarves, hats and gloves. Jay starts moving. He holds one of his mittens between his teeth while slipping on the other. They are the fingerless type – for greater manipulation.

He strides down the dark corridor.

– On my way, I say.

I jog to catch up with him. We enter the kitchen. The fluorescent lights are on. The room is L-shaped. In this long part machines hum. Work surfaces gleam. I think of my own smaller, warmer kitchen. My stomach feels empty. I chide myself: play first, breakfast later.

We turn into the short part. Mrs. Sherman is sitting at the table. She is studying some files. Jay's lawyer mother. So fond of mine.

– And where are you boys going?, she says calmly, without looking up.

– We have some tobogganing to do, mother.

She raises her head and looks at me.

– And whose idea is this?, she says with a little smile.

– Jay's, I blurt out. . . And mine.

– I see, Mrs. Sherman pronounces. Well, I want you two back here in half an hour. I have things for you to do.

Jay looks at his shatter-proof watch and gives a curt nod. His mother resumes reading her files. We walk to the side door. Jay opens it and goes out first.

Outside the air is startling. I feel giddy.

Yes – let's go and do it.

I glance shyly at the sky: clearing. My mother will come tomorrow. I'll protest, of course.

Jay has darted off to my left. He's walking briskly across the driveway toward the garage. I'm about to follow him when I notice another fresh set of tracks; these ones leading off to my right. They curve around the driveway to the front side of the house.

– Jay, whose footprints are those?

He stops and about turns. He looks to where I'm pointing and says:

– Dad's – who else's?

– Where's he gone?

– Work – where else?

– Work? But my Dad said on the phone last night no-one was expected in today.

– Well, when you're the boss you gotta do more than what's expected.

I imagine my father – Mr. Sherman's right-hand man – slumbering safely. I look at the footprints again.

– But how's he going to get there?

Jay shrugs his shoulders.

– Maybe he'll walk. C'mon, he says, turning on his heel.

I follow. Jay reaches the garage. He raises the door in one fluid action.

– Just wait here, he says over his shoulder.

I wait for him. I look back across the driveway. Trees obscure the view of land and sea.

Jay re-emerges.

– Here she is, he announces.

In his hands he displays a white baby bath, made of hard plastic; rectangular with rounded edges and a curved rim. It has a flat bottom which slants forward near one end. On its side there's a small colour ABC design. His youngest sister's baby bath. The Shermans never throw anything out.

I say nothing. Last night this all sounded better. Jay stares at me and says:

– Well?

– Well. . . I don't know, Jay.

– What don't you know?

– Now that I see it. . . are you sure it's safe?

– Hey, I've told you, it'll work a treat. What's the matter with you?

– Nothing.

– Okay, Let's go then. No time to waste.

He marches past me. He takes long strides across the driveway, carrying the bath in one hand. His path merges with his father's.

– Wait a sec, Jay.

He halts, half-turns and stares impatiently. I jog through the snow. As soon as I draw level he springs into his rhythm again. I manage to keep pace.

As we're walking past the front of the house Jay puts a hand on my shoulder and says:

– You see, the thing you gotta learn is: how to get the things you want to get done done with the things you got.

– Bricolage.

– What?

– The French call that bricolage.

– Right. Anyway, to survive you gotta improvise; that's what my old man says. The toboggan I had back home was the *best*. But this will do, this will do.

We come to the front gates. Jay opens one and walks through first. Once I have followed him he closes it behind me.

After the rattle I'm unnerved by the silence for the first time. I feel sealed in silence.

The road is ours. We're first. We've won our private contest. I think of breakfast again. Jay surveys the run; hands on hips, bath at his feet.

I too look down the steep gradient; try to work things out. It must be sixty, seventy metres to the road bridge. It can be seen from here despite the bend some two-thirds of the way down. Seen clearly – its granite walls topped with snow.

The beautiful bridge, the steep road.

It seems even colder out here. I turn and look back through the black bars of the gates. Gothic pile – that's what my father calls it. Gothic pile – yes, it sounds just right. Jay's family have occupied it since the corporation brought his father in. I look up at the alcove window and think of the telescope.

I wish I were watching this.

– Well? Jay says smoothly.

– You think this is the right place?

– I sure do.

– Not too high up?

– No way. This is gonna be a mean ride! Look at that curve!

– What about stopping?

– Would you just look straight for once? The incline starts even before the bridge. No problem.

– Oh yes, yes, I see.

Jay crouches at the side of the pavement and runs his fingertips over the ice.

– Love it, love it, he whispers.

He stands, picks up the bath and steps onto the road. He walks steadily to the centre. There he places the bath – upside down, slant end forward – and sits on it. He plants his feet and arched hands on the ice, leaning back a little. His leg obscures the ABC – a pity, it's what I like best about our toboggan.

I want to call out to him. I don't know what – tell him to wait for me or to come back, I don't know. But it doesn't matter. I can't say anything. Not now. He has his eyes fixed on the road ahead. His hawk-like eyes.

He begins to move the bath back and forth beneath him. He raises his feet and tucks them against the sides; continuing to slide faster and faster with his hands alone.

He pushes off. He thunders down the road; hunching forward, placing his hands just behind his feet. He picks up speed relentlessly but holds to the centre. He tilts his body as he reaches the bend. He takes it well and rights himself. But then he leans back a little. The bath starts to turn; but he's on the incline already. Reaching the bridge he puts his feet out. They dampen his speed even further.

As soon as the bath stops Jay stands up. He looks back up the hill. I wave. He turns away. He steps onto the pavement, leans his hands against the low wall and looks down the railway line.

Moments pass. I long to know what he's thinking. He turns and walks back to the bath. He picks it up and slings it over his shoulder.

I am tempted to go and meet him as he climbs up the pavement; but I stay near the gates. I stand very still. I want to be invisible. A mad thought.

As he nears I can see his expression is one of cool pride.

– Jay, you made that look easy!

He does not respond until he reaches the gates:

– Jus' nothing, he mumbles.

We look at each other, Jay's grey eyes blank.

– So! I say.

– So! he mimics.

The silence resumes. There is nothing I can say to my friend. I look down at my shoes. Paratroop boots crunch into the white ground in front of them. I look up. Our steamy breaths rise in the narrow space between our faces.

– Your turn, m'man.

I step back and lean against the gates.

– Maybe you should do it one more time; so as I can study your technique even closer.

– That's not necessary.

– Don't you want to do it again?

– Your turn, he smiles politely.

– . . . I don't really want to.

Jay takes a step backward.

– Jesus! he says. Jesus Christ! Last night it was all "great, Jay", "cool, Jay", "let's do it, Jay" – what's this?

– I don't see the point. We know we got here first. We know it can be done.

– What we know is that you're chickenshit.

I do not respond. His mouth distorts.

– Chickenshit, he growls slowly.

I inhale sharply and ask:

– What's the point?

Jay drops the bath in front of my feet. I do nothing. He sighs and says:

– It's not for me. Don't you see that? It's to prove something to yourself!

– Prove what?

He thinks for a moment and then says forcefully:

– That you can do it!

– It?

– Yeah!

He comes forward, picks up the bath and offers it to me.

– Aw come on! he says, with equal weight on the last two words.

I take the bath.

I stand at the edge of the pavement, thinking hard about control. I look down at the ice and step onto it.

It's alive. I concentrate as hard as I can. I make cautious progress. No problem. I look ahead to where Jay placed the bath. I slip. I let the bath go. My hands break my fall. They are rewarded with a dull burn. Water invades my gloves and trousers.

I know he is smiling. I can't turn around. I get up and steady myself. I pick up the bath gingerly. I proceed to the centre. I put the bath down and sit on it; positioning myself as I remember Jay did. Good, Muiris. I look up.

The ice-covered road is smooth and beautiful indeed. I can see a good portion of the bridge as well. I could look at this all morning. I hear Jay's voice:

– Jus' keep the balance, the balance.

I turn my head and nod stiffly. I face forward again. Control, Muiris. I feel the bath making tiny movements beneath me.

– Tell ya what! Let me give ya a push!

I turn my head once more and open my mouth. But nothing comes. Jay has stomped out onto the ice already. He walks around behind me.

– Position feet and hands, I hear him grunt.

I do so. The bath inches forward.

There is a thud of palms against my spine.

The bath rumbles forward. It picks up speed at a rate that makes me whimper. Branches and gate posts fly past, yet I've never seen such sharp, fierce shapes. I'm in crazy time. My legs are stiff. I'm off centre and the bend's approaching. I remember: control. I lean my body. My angle changes enough for me to survive. The bridge looms. I right myself in one jerk. The bath begins to spin. A spin that will never end. A spin with me in it, yes; but surely I'm watching this somewhere. The incline begins. I'm looking at the wall. I need to slow faster in this forever. I put a foot out. Ice-flakes fly. I could count them. I'm flipped off the bath. I'm head over heels – suspended in an instant. I hear the bath bounce on the ice like the beat of a drum. My head hits the ground with a muffled sound. My legs are bent up against the wall. I am staring at the sky. Staring at the night sky, yes. With my telescope. Tracking the stars as they move. In their time. At their own secret speed.

LA PARISIENNE

Leena Dhingra

LA PARISIENNE

The fact that the Duchess should also disappear at this very same time, that felt somehow ominous. She was one of those people who was always there! Could it mean something?

Maya climbed out of the dark Metro and brought her brooding thoughts into the spring sunlight. The Place de L'Etoile was awash in it. Everything sparkled. The trees in blossom. The newly cleaned stones of the Arc de Triomphe. The swirling cars reflecting the sun: short sharp sparklers. Maya looked around at the familiar scene, breathing it in and snap shutting her eyes as if to imprint it in her head. The image of the Arc glowed red.

It was not unusual for Maya to greet Paris, she did this frequently, every time she came home for the holidays. But this time there was a difference, an intensity, coming from the sudden realisation that she might have to leave it, that it might not remain the home to which she regularly returned.

This holiday had been full of unexpected developments. She had come to spend the usual Easter holidays. First, The Duchess disappeared, then her mother was called away to nurse a sick relative in Switzerland. And now her father had to leave for India where he had been offered an important job which he needed to decide about. Maya had just left him at the air terminal, and was still confused by the implications of this sudden journey.

"Papa. If you take this job in India," she'd asked, "does it mean we'll actually leave Paris?" From her father's look, she realised there must have been a tone of incredulity in her voice. Her father's reply was tender. "Well, yes, eventually. We'll go home. Wouldn't you like that?"

Home was always a difficult idea. She tried to grapple with it as she swiftly strode down the Avenue MacMahon, falling into a familiar pace and counting: one, two, three. Nine hundred and thirty three steps would bring her to the apartment block of her Paris 'home'. In London, there was 'home', flat shares and bed-sits which changed once a year, often more. And then there was India, where they all went together for 'home leave', but always stayed as guests in other people's homes. Of course India was 'proper' home, like family and ancient origins and ancestors. But the home she'd always known was Paris. She couldn't even remember not speaking French.

She stopped at the intersection. Paris, she whispered, the city of my childhood. And this is my *quartier*, my patch. Stuffed full of memories. Home for more than half my life! My childhood belongs to this city! How can I just leave it?

She looked around at the familiar cafés and shops. Rosine was standing at the entrance of her music shop and looking across the street to just beyond where Maya was. Maya knew exactly where her gaze rested and turned to look herself at the central table on the terrace of Le Vigier, the imposing corner café behind her. The table was empty. The Duchess was not there. Maya turned back to look at Rosine who waved, beckoning her to cross over.

Maya negotiated her way through the traffic. She was quite adept at it. After all, ten years in this *quartier*, she counted as she dodged through the cars, fifteen since she'd arrived in Paris at the age of four, which was more than three quarters of her life so far – she knew the ways of the city.

"*Salut*, Rosine," she called, hopping on to the pavement.

"*Salut*, Maya. Your father left okay?" They greeted each other with the mandatory three kisses. "Look!" said Rosine, and they both turned towards the terrace of Le Vigier. "Still no Duchess." Rosine shook her head. "That's ten days no-one has seen her."

"I know." Maya nodded her head thoughtfully. "Everything seems to have gone funny since she disappeared. Do you think she might come back before I leave?"

"When's that?"

"In five days. My term starts on Monday."

"Who knows?" Rosine shrugged her shoulders philosophically. "I never knew I would be so affected by her disappearance. It's just that she's always been there!"

They both looked across the street. Rosine's shop, usually filled with music, was silent.

"We might leave Paris, you know," said Maya wistfully.

Rosine gave Maya a nudge and a wink. "Tell you what. I'll shut shop and we'll have a coffee. And imagine! You've got five days for yourself! You can have a ball!"

Maya watched Rosine pull down the grille of her shop, which was not much more than a narrow corridor lined high with records of every description. Two people could barely stand alongside. But Rosine was something of an expert on music and had a very faithful, select clientele. She would sit at the back of her shop on a step ladder next to the hi-fi filling the shop and street with beautiful music from her carefully chosen selection. She always dressed in the same way: black or dark navy trousers and sweaters and a bright silk scarf around her neck. Her dark hair was cut very short and she never wore make-up. She hung the blackboard and chalked the message of where she was to be found.

"Come. Let's go." She slipped her arm into Maya's and they crossed the street.

"Did I tell you that I found out the name of the Duchess?" enquired Rosine in between calling out the order for the coffees.

"No. You didn't. What is it?"

"Well, my dear. It's Madame Verlaine. That's the only thing I've been able to find out. And where she lives. I'm going to go there tomorrow."

"Verlaine! Do you think she could be related to the poet?"

"She could at that."

"She is quite poetic in her own way." Maya tried to remember the words of one of his poems, about the couple in the park.

The Duchess was one of the local colourfuls, colourful in every way. Her dyed red hair was piled high on her head and lacquered into a dome, and wisps of curls framed her heavily made-up face. Her lipstick always clashed with her hair. She would stride down the street, gently swinging an umbrella, or a parasol in summer, nodding majestically at the odd greeting. Nobody stared, she was just part of the scene, part of *l'habitude*, the usual.

Whatever the weather, she invariably appeared every afternoon. Around fifteen hundred hours, *Madame la Duchesse* would walk down the Avenue de Ternes, into the Café Le Vigier and seat herself at a table near the plate glass front from where she could survey the scene. She would stay there some two or three hours, mostly alone, but occasionally joined by someone for a short while. Sometimes, she would come twice a day, for breakfast as well.

"What I find altogether *extraordinaire*," declared Rosine, "is that someone so familiar, whom one has seen almost every day for years, whom everyone seems to know, should simply disappear – and then one discovers that no-one knows anything about her."

She shrugged her shoulders, shook her head, waved her arms, and let fly: *zut, flute* and *merde* all over the place. The familiar gesticulations and intonations of Parisian life which Maya knew so well and immediately assumed on stepping foot in Calais.

"But Rosine. It's not just everyone else. We never bothered to find out anything about her, or to talk to her."

"It didn't seem necessary as long as she was there."

"Yes. I suppose that's the way I feel about Paris. It's always just been there."

The Duchess was a nickname Rosine had invented. There were others: One of the *garçons* at Le Vigier was called *Le Loup*, the Wolf, because of his long sideburns and hungry eager lips. Others were The Crab, The Rose, Oscar *le Canard*: Oscar The Duck. And of course *La Duchesse*, The Duchess. She was special. And now she had disappeared.

"But don't you find it *innouie*, unheard of, that no-one knows anything about her? It's as if she were a figure in a dream. A figment of the imagination! An illusion."

"That's what Maya means, you know. Illusion." ventured Maya.

"Let's have another coffee, or the illusion of one." Rosine winked as she waved for attention.

"I'd prefer a chocolate." Drinking small black coffees was a 'grown-up' taste she was trying to acquire. A chocolate was more comforting and she needed that now.

"Everything's been unexpected this holiday, people disappearing and all. And now, Paris might even disappear." Maya stirred her chocolate.

"*Allez*, Mayou." Rosine gave her a gentle thump. "Paris will always be there, and in any case, you will always be a *Parisienne!*"

"And after?"

Rosine flung her arms into the air. "And after. . . and after. . . and what does it matter! Whether you go to Bombay or Bankok, Paris is a part of you! *Il n'y a plus d'apres*, 'There is no after'," Rosine started to sing the famous song by Juliette Greco.

Maya completed the verse: "*Il n'y a qu'aujourdhui*, 'There is only today'."

They left the café singing. The patron smiled approvingly.

"What will you do over these five days?" Rosine pulled up the grille of her shop.

"Wander around. Be a tourist. Visit places. And also I told papa I would clean the apartment."

"Be sure to come by morning and afternoon so I can tell you the news and we can have a coffee."

They kissed each other goodbye. "A *demain*."

Rosine perched herself hawk-like on her stool. Albinoni's 'Adagio' caught Maya's ears as she turned the corner.

Maya strolled through the market and bought a few provisions on her way home. She tried to recall various stories she knew about different stallholders, told to her either by Rosine or Mme Nicole.

Mme Nicole was the concierge of the apartment building, and concierges were notorious for knowing, gossiping, interfering. They would gather together on the benches of the tree-lined avenues, shake their fingers, and wag their chins. They were like terrorizing spiders with their network of webs across the city in which to catch the hapless tenants. Every Parisian knew they had to be humoured. In fact it was one of her father's last instructions to Maya as he'd boarded the airport bus.

"Remember Madame Nicole. Be respectful and polite and get her a bunch of flowers before you go."

"But you just gave her some, papa."

"Doesn't matter, you give her some more. If you need more money get some from Jacques. He'll call anyway."

Maya pressed the buzzer to open the main door. Mme Nicole saw her coming in through the glazed door of her flat and rose to meet her. There would be no escape this time.

"*Bonjour, mon poulet.*"

Fancy being called a hen as a term of endearment, thought Maya as she kissed Mme Nicole for the second time that day.

"So your father's gone now and you're all alone, *ma cherie.* Come in and sit with us."

Maya managed to escape, saying she was expecting a telephone call, and ran up the four flights of stairs to the apartment.

The apartment was small: a large studio comprising two rooms broken into one, a comfortable kitchen large enough to eat in and a bathroom. But it was beautiful: bright and sunny and full of character. Her father's many books lined the walls and her mother's curios, lacquered Chinese furniture, Kashmir shawls, Thai Buddhas, and Tibetan Thankas adorned the place. Maya walked around. She looked at the little Persian rug by the bed and remembered its arrival: her mother had bought it urgently one day to hide a fresh iron scald from her father! The rug blended in with the many rich ochres, maroons and blues of the room. Her father had noticed nothing and Maya and her mother had exchanged sly smiles. Later, when she ironed, she would roll the rug to one side, so that by now what lay underneath had multiple marks.

Maya picked up a large embossed Munich beer mug with a lid

and shook it. Coins jingled. Her 'refugee mug'! She remembered what her mother used to say: "Keep an open hand and good fortune will flow, but a clenched fist will damage your soul." From an early age Maya had been encouraged to put away part of her pocket money for refugees who had been less fortunate than her family. "Some people," her mother would tell her, "lost everything when India was Partitioned, and the best way to give thanks for what you have is to share." Now the mug was full of foreign money: German, Dutch, English, Italian, Belgian, Swiss, Cambodian, Indian – her father should have taken that.

She returned the mug to its place on the Tibetan dresser and looked around at the flat, thinking how much she loved it. She sat down on the shawl-covered bed to contemplate the room. Everything was so familiar: the benign Buddha head behind which she hid her sweets, above it Reorich's mystic Tibetan mountains, purple in the pink-red glow of the setting sun. The many books, in many languages, always in the same places. In her eyeline was *The Naked And The Dead*, in the same place for the last ten years. For her father, a new rug might pass unnoticed for a while, but a misplaced book would immediately be sensed. Suddenly, sitting there, the apartment took on an aspect she had never seen before. Around her she saw the different ways in which each of her parents had dealt with their loss and the uprooting from their home, their city, their dreams, and even their country following the Partition of India. Her father had looked to the life of the mind, seeking both refuge and meaning in books, ideas, literature, philosophy, and the cosmopolitan cultural life of the city. Her mother's way was more pragmatic, and to be found in the *Marche aux Puces*, The Flea Market, to which she would go regularly to seek out discarded Imperial loot, particularly the magnificent shawls from Kashmir, so very rare and highly prized in India, yet available in unappreciated abundance at the flea market. One day, all would be returned to where it rightfully belonged.

"We'll go home. Wouldn't you like that?" Her father had said. The tenderness in his voice took on a new dimension. Going home, she thought must have a different meaning for them. She felt confused, as though she needed to make sense of something, but didn't know what. She looked round the flat as though to find it.

Maya is illusion. Brahman the sole reality, the Universal self, beyond space, time and form. Atman, the individual self. Moksha is liberation, that realisation. She had heard all these words discussed in the flat. But what did they all mean? Even the word 'home': what and where was home?

She looked at the gilded Buddha on the mantlepiece. It did not reply, but its raised hand, she knew, signified: do not fear.

In the morning, Jacques telephoned: did she need anything and what was she planning to do?

"Roam the city on your own!" He laughed. "And why not, after all? But I can take you out to dinner once, no? A Parisian dinner. What about Friday? Dress nicely and meet me downstairs at eight."

On the Chinese bureau, next to her father's list of chores to be completed before she left for London, he had also left a pile of Metro and bus tickets. Enough to travel around non-stop! she thought. She put on a record of Yves Montand's 'Paris' as she got ready and decided where to go first.

Montmartre was her first stop. At the Rue St Vincent, she started to sing 'Les Escaliers De La Butte', where according to the song the poet met an unknown street girl, loved her, lost her and composed this song in the hope that she would hear it. "Princess of the street, be welcome in my wounded heart." She climbed up the steps to the Sacre Coeur, and bought a pretty picture in pastels and golds of the Holy Family.

Rosine winced. "Why on earth did you buy that?"

Maya shrugged. "Felt like it. I remembered when I was in the local school all my friends would have their Communion and get these pretty cards and I wished I had one. So I bought one!"

"You should have told me. I'd have given you all mine. You can have them now if I haven't thrown them all away!"

But of the Duchess there was no news. Rosine had been to the house but the concierge was away, and the replacement didn't know anything.

Paris was celebrated in so many songs that wherever Maya went she remembered an appropriate melody and soon these guided her forays into the city. Her favourite was the one about the river itself on its journey to the city; first it flowed, then it rolled, but on reaching Paris, it sang. It sang, and sang and sang, day and night, for the Seine was a lover and Paris, her beloved.

On Friday she cleaned the apartment lovingly, accompanied by Yves Montand, Charles Trenet, Jacques Brel, Juliette Greco and Edith Piaf. In the afternoon she went for her usual coffee with Rosine. But by now they were both becoming philosophical.

"*Merde!*" exclaimed Rosine, running her fingers through her short hair. "Everything changes and passes in the end. But somehow I feel she will be back. The Wolf is certain she will. I will write to you in London and tell you."

In the evening she got out of her jeans and into a sari. Jacques gave her an approving look and instead of the usual familiar three pecks on the cheek, he kissed her hand and opened the car door.

"What have you been doing?"

"This and that. Today I cleaned the flat and yesterday I went to see the Guignol."

Jacques laughed. "What, the marionettes for the little ones? Why?"

Maya shrugged. "*Comme ça.* Just like that. It's the Paris of my childhood."

"Well, tonight I am taking you for a worldly dinner. You are no longer a little one."

They drove to a club in the heart of St Germain, small but chic.

"And not American!" Jacques informed her. "I told your father I would look after you, in my way, take you to a good night club."

"What did he say?"

Jacques laughed. "Ha! Maybe he did not believe me! Ah la la! Your parents live in dreams. Someone has to educate you into the ways of the world."

Jacques gave the order as the floorshow started. A tall, beautiful, and well built blonde came on to the sound of Peggy Lee's 'Fever' and started to dance her clothes off to cool from the heat of an imaginary sun.

"The song's American."

Jacques shrugged his shoulders in mock despair. Maya turned away as the woman shed her bra. As the dinner arrived Jacques leaned over "*Bon appetit.*"

"Is this supposed to give one an appetite?"

"But of course! Really, Maya. You are so very English. It is worrying. I keep telling your father. It must be changed!"

"I don't see your logic. I'm sitting here in a sari, talking to you in French, so why and how should I be more English than anything else?" Maya protested.

Jacques threw up his hands. "*Exactement* ! That is *la tragedie.*"

"Does Papa come here?" Maya was taken aback by his censorious tone.

"Yes, if I invite him." He winked.

Maya was not sure whether he was teasing or not.

The floor show ended, the lights dimmed and the room filled with soft dance music.

"You see Maya, you will be twenty this year, a young woman and no longer a young girl. There is much to learn to become a woman."

"And you're going to teach me, yes?"

"Yes. What I can." He poured some more wine and told her how to taste it. "Now, what would you say if I told you that the *danseuse* was not a woman, but a man?"

"Are you trying to make fun of me?" retorted Maya aggressively.

"*Allez,* Mayoushka! English again! *Non, ma cherie!* Why should I want to make fun of you? I have seen you grow up. And now we are having a delicious dinner in grown-up Paris. And I am telling you the truth. It was not a woman. It was a man."

Mayoushka was what he'd called her when she was younger. Maya relaxed. She looked around her. Grown-up Paris.

"So this is like the Guignol of the adults."

Jacques threw his head back with laughter. "Yes! *Le Guignol des grands*! I must remember that." He poured some more wine.

Maya looked around her smiling widely. The *garçon* bowed. Paris! What a nice place to be. "Thank you for bringing me here."

"The pleasure is mine. Shall we dance?" He held out his hand. She took it and slipped into his arms.

The next morning was departure day. The flat gleamed, spotless. Maya felt strange. There was nothing left to do except the flowers for Mme Nicole. She'd have breakfast on the terrace of Le Vigier and buy them on her return. On the desk she double-checked her father's list and folded it. It had writing on the back with a line through it. A poem he had been working on.

> "We met, we pass,
> We pause, or turn again,
> A moment stay, then blindly journey on.
> Little we know of others,
> Much of none,
> The secret self, in them
> In us, unwon."

She read it again, folded the paper and put it in her pocket. In the café she ordered a hot chocolate and a croissant. The Wolf served her. She looked absently at the street, her *quartier*, her patch. The city of her childhood. A childhood which was now over. Disappeared. Like The Duchess. She looked across to Rosine's shop, but she had not yet arrived. She felt alone and vulnerable. Around her the café buzzed. She dipped her croissant into the chocolate. Behind her The Wolf greeted a customer.

"Ah, Madame. We have missed you. The usual."

"The usual," came the reply.

"You have been away," came another voice.

"Yes. I was suddenly called out of Paris. A young cousin was to become a nun."

"Ah! Really!"

"I am all she has, so I went to be with her. They get married, you know. A proper ceremony. A gold ring. They get married to Jesus. So you could say that now Jesus was my cousin-in-law!"

Maya spluttered on her chocolate as it went down the wrong way. She shook her head. Did she really hear that? Who said it? She turned. The Duchess! The Duchess was sitting there!

Maya felt paralysed. It felt as if the blood had drained from her body. For a while she could neither think nor move. She smiled inanely. Finally, feeling a little better, she got up to leave. The Duchess was sitting on her own, in front of her a large bowl of *café au lait*.

Maya collected herself and walked slowly. As she passed The Duchess' table she paused. *"Bonjour*, Madame Verlaine." Her voice rang out.

The Duchess looked at her, shocked, surprised and then pleased. She smiled and inclined her head to the side. *"Bonjour*, Mademoiselle Maya."

Maya walked home on air. Her smile was so wide, it hurt. Just like the time she first arrived in Paris at the age of four. She bought a huge bunch of flowers for Mme Nicole, and a box of chocolates as well. She then rushed to Rosine's.

The Duchess was no longer on the terrace. Maya stormed into the shop.

"Rosine! Rosine! She's come back. She's there! I saw her. The Duchess. She's come back!" Rosine looked stupefied. They fell into each other's arms. "And Rosine! I spoke to her! She knows my name!"

From the train Maya watched the city disappear. Like her childhood, it had gone. Dissolved. Illusion. Maya! She was now a grown up. And since her childhood would always be a part of her, so too would Paris. She smiled. Yes, a bit of her would always remain a – *Parisienne*.

AND EVERYTHING GOES TO HELL

by Francis Gilbert

Screaming, screaming, screaming.

I swear something seems to be breaking out of the tracks, the walls, the platform, the tunnel, the waste-paper bins and the sagging billboards.

My eardrums are bursting as the woman's screeching meshes with the onslaught of the train.

It bellows and lumbers through the wire-streaming tunnel. The driver's carriage has barely entered the station when it's clear the body is bolting along the very edge of the platform with the intention of catching the precise moment of electric impact between wheel and track on her head.

A dispersed row of commuters shouts, and wave their hands uselessly. The dirty metal lines crackle violently.

I stuff my fingers in my ears. Brightly lit windows are zipping silently past me. I'm clinging onto a prayer the Aboriginals sang when the white man mowed them down:

May no bad things arise from the crust of the earth

But still the screaming twists amidst the sea-shell sounds in my ear. I have to look. There's a hideous voyeur inside that forces me to look. I feel my body flinching, quivering with adrenalin, anticipating her excruciating pain.

I see her gathering herself together like an expert, high-board diver, tightening the muscles into a composed, compact unit, bowing her head, clasping her hands together as if in prayer, and bracing herself to dive towards the dusty silver space between the train and the tunnel.

Dry, constricting gusts of wind whip my face. I shut my eyes so fiercely that a blood-red light spills from my forehead.

And then the noises stop simultaneously.

The pounding quietens in my head. I open my eyes. The windows slow-mo before me. I turn to face the worst; a dead body and a hopelessly delayed train.

But a young businessman has seized her in a vice-like grip. He is dragging her away from the precipice towards the swivelling video camera, perched above the vandalised alcove. A pale, stricken urgency is punched through his face. We all look up at the camera for help. Perhaps someone will see us in the monitoring room and have pity.

People jostle around her, vying for a glimpse of her distress. I wish that I had my camera to capture their excitement, their hypocrisy. Some put their spidery fingers across their mouths in disappointment. She is physically unharmed. She isn't even worth an anecdote.

I am reminded of the lost souls Dante speaks about in the outer circle of hell, who lived their lives without praise or blame. I can almost see the metaphoric wasps and horseflies gnawing at their faces, the avenging worms gobbling up their false tears.

It's at moments of spiritual desolation like these that I'm glad that I have my mythological map to refer back to. This is what saves me from being one of Dante's apathetic inhabitants of Hell. The map that I am creating means no-one's tragedy goes unnoted and the whole of the city's horror is charted. Her brief torment will have a suitable place amongst the mythology I am drawing up for the metropolis.

This will be my first suicide attempt to etch in for the King's Cross Tube Station.

She is slumped, floppy as a lover, in his arms. Her red hair is tousled against his immaculately cut sleeves.

The crowd anxiously scrutinise her reaction to the presence of the train. She remains motionless, her eyes shut, her body as drained as Michelangelo's deflated man.

We are encouraged by her lifelessness. She doesn't look like she would try anything stupid again. Or at least not today.

And so the rickety train begins to suck them in like dust to a vacuum cleaner. The businessman winces. Crowsfeet spread around his eyes, under the effort of deciding what to do. His face soon composes itself. He promptly leaves her on an eaten bench and hops on the train.

But the girl's suicide attempt has too many implications for me to abandon her. I realise why I have felt drawn to this plat-form, of all the platforms I could choose from. There was a larger, more meaningful plan behind it all: it was to enable me to complete the map!

I need to know if she's aware of being a sacrificial victim, what symbols she is drawn to, what Gods she sees in her distress.

Conditions are perfect: the platform is as deserted and windswept as the Sahara.

I am the only living thing beside her. The camera, like an arthritic raven, whirrs and creaks from its vantage point, focus-sing on us. She is slowly unscrunching her eyes, her hand shield-ing her from what she might see. Her fingers cast bands of shadow across her nose and mouth. She takes her hands from her cheeks. In the few minutes of having left her on the bench, her body has recovered itself miraculously. A ruddy colour has re-invigorated her cheeks.

Her face blazes at me. It has the most exquisite architecture. Hollowed cheekbones, deep, deep blue eyes, flaming red hair.

Is she a Persphone, an Ariadne, or a Eurydice?

Generally I find that most extraordinary women of the Underground do fit into one of these three mythical sub-sections. For the purposes of my map I take my cue from Greek mythology because it has the best charting of the Underworld.

She begins to shake off her dreamy, dazed expression. She sticks her hands like a diviner through the soupy yellow air. Tears and Underground dust have matted her long, red hair. The re-invigorating colour has become a fierce heat. Sweat dribbles down from her temples and the sides of her red cheeks.

I pull her up from her slouched position on the bench. I dust off the grime from her cream chiffon blouse, and off the knee caps of her loose, silky trousers. I pull her loose rain-coat over her shoulders. She begins to look like the cultured lady that she no doubt is (in between suicide attempts).

She leans her head against the inside of the crumbling alcove. I am unsure what to do. I have never interviewed one of my mythological characters before. I tend just to photograph them or note them down in my mind, and work out from meagre physical information what place they will have in my map. I scan the platform for the Guard again.

She opens her eyes. I check myself, crouch beside her and do my best to look confident and reassuring.

She detects my unease immediately. Her hand reaches out and touches the cold tiles. There is something distinctly unhinged about the way she runs the tips of her fingers down the wall. She is caressing the grafittied brick like a long lost husband. Perhaps subconsciously she is actually besotted by the King of the Underworld, Hades?

Snot-like slime drips down the cracked, curving plaster above us. Indeed we could be stuck up Hades' diseased nostril. My intuition tells me the situation is hopeless. Ultimately the Underworld is going to claim us all.

She sees me staring above her alcove. She leans out of the dark green shadow and cranes her neck to see the cracked ceiling. The pasty electric light hits her cheeks, her large, neurotic eyes, her blood-red lips. I feel another pang for her painful beauty.

I struggle to think of something to say. What can I say, though? That it is nice day to commit suicide on?

In my desperation, I resort to talking about my interest in the video tapes that the underground controllers keep. I've managed to get hold of a number of them. I find them the most fascinating things to watch because they tell you more about people and places than the arts or sciences ever could. If you watch them long enough you can see the areas and things that people are most subconsciously attracted to. The sacred places, the domains of power, the evil objects, the good objects.

Then I start chuntering on about my specialist studies which take me all around the innards of London. I am convinced that I am taking her mind off her own troubles. My delivery is rather hysterical and nervous but she is listening to me.

Her head inclines like a child drifting off to a bedtime story. She has stopped sweating. Her lower lip is quivering. But my mad talking is calming her. She rests her head back into the sickly shadows and takes a deep breath. She doesn't attempt to dam my gibbering flow of words until she says:

"Please forgive me, and my terrible presumption. I am fully

aware that you're in a state of shock."

Her voice is soft and intuitive. She is exceptionally well-spoken. Her sentence suggests a precision and controlled syntax which would have done Athena proud.

Her words make me conscious of my extreme insensitivity. I look for the Guard again. I just want to go home and smother myself in the security of drafting up the map. I'm embarrassed that I have just divulged a great deal of my personal life to a total stranger.

She seems too preoccupied to really understand the full magnitude of what I have said. In a way I am rather pleased. It saves me the embarrassment of having to explain myself.

I take her clinically by the hand. I am decided that I am going to help her and have done with it. I drag her away from the lethal tracks. Her tensed, resisting body tells me that she doesn't want to leave the comforting glint of the runners.

"There's absolutely no reason why you should be putting yourself out on my behalf. I have been fully independent for a number of years now."

She says this in such a weak, shivery way that I'm not convinced. She does actually need me. I feel heartened; by making her part of my project, I am helping her. She could well be a Persephone: she is in love with Hades and at the same time she is debilitated by his hideous tyranny.

I pull her to the escalator and let go of her. The imprint of her small warm hand lingers. Its a long time since anyone held me like that. I think it's strange that she's wearing a subtle, musky scent . Did she want to be a sweet-smelling corpse? Did she want to prove her sophistocation to those who found her?

I wonder if I should cart her to the police station or the hospital. I think about asking her, and then decide against it. She seems above such things. I'll take her to the surface and have done with it. I'll be Hermes, the messenger of the Gods, and she'll be my Eurydice. I am no Orpheus.

She is silent as we glide up the dirty silver escalator. She stares at the glossy advertisements with the intensity of an electric drill. She doesn't look ahead at all. I'm standing behind her, preventing her from bolting back into Hades' arms. She seems to resent me barring her way back. She puts her hands into her luxurious coat's big pockets, and punches at the patterned lining.

With a creaking jerk of the head, she turns round to me and asks:

"Have you ever fucked anyone?"

I squirm. I almost want to laugh because her question is so aristocratically enunciated. But I can't. Her words are so vacant and abstract. She could be asking me about the weather. Admittedly she's hit me on one of my weaker points; I have never enjoyed such pleasures, though this doesn't seem to be such a bad thing these days. Nevertheless I am rather offended by the question.

"Are you providing this excellent chaperone service because you want to fuck me?" she persists vindictively.

She buttons her billowing coat up to the collar, and stands obstinately before the metal ticket cabinets, refusing to budge. Her imperiousness makes me conscious of the shabby clothes I'm wearing.

I decide I've taken her as far as the barrier and I've done my bit. I break into a fast walk and try to lose her. I kick myself for being so deceived about her in the first place. She's probably a sluttish Helen of Troy, or even an Aphrodite straying into the nether regions. There's no way she's got the purity of a Persephone, an Ariadne or a Eurydice.

I pass through the ticket barrier, and head towards the release of my map. I'll be able to mark in the region of the Suicidal Madam. But my thoughts are disrupted immediately by a commotion at the ticket barrier. It is her again, she is screaming at the tired, sunken ticket man (a spiritless Charon):

"Let me through, let me through! Can't you see that I'm not just any old common woman of the streets? "

"But you haven't got a ticket!" He says irritably.

Instinctively I rush back, and give him the money for the ticket. I don't so much as glance at her. She hovers behind my shoulder, wilting a little bit in her expensive clothes. She thanks me rather mournfully. She seems to have changed a little bit. There isn't the same defiance, or malevolence in her. She almost seems sane. Apologies gush out of her. She is sorry for offending me, and she can tell that I'm not the sort of chap who is going to rape her. I nod gravely, accepting what she says.

I turn to leave her but she won't stop apologising. She will blame herself for the rest of her life for offending me. It will bug her forever. I just want to be left alone. I want to breathe the fresh underground air of my map. The constant flux of people under low, starkly-lit ceilings is oppressing me.

I hurry out of the subway. I breath in the cold mouldy-fresh air and wince under the horror of confronting the daylight.

I am blinded by sharp, spluttering rays of sun. A crystalline blue sky shrouds the blackened Victorian edifices of King's Cross. The average load of dossers, prostitutes, pimps and drug dealers shift on their feet, intermingling between businessmen and road-sweepers.

How I hate the sunlight and all its attendant realities! How despicably smug and falsely optimistic it seems to be! It reeks of the avenging Sun God that would attempt to wipe out all the Moon Deities and the beautiful Underground Goddesses!

I can hardly open my eyes. I am compelled to crouch down and scrutinise the frosted litter that flies around the pavement in chaotic vortices. I put on my sunglasses that I always wear in the daylight, even if the sky is admirably smothered in the blackest gloom.

I shuffle as quickly away from the hooligan sunlight as I can. But my fast exit is soon halted. I get a nasty shock.

She has been following me. There is a girlish skip in her step as she tries to keep up. She is breathless, telling me that she just wants someone to talk to. She stops outside the blackened window of a pornographer's and says she doesn't know many characters in the city. I think about how easily she could be exploited. But when I see the contemptuous sneer she gives the seedy, spattered window, I have my suspicions that she is a good deal sharper and street-wise than I first supposed.

It strikes me that she wasn't trying to commit suicide in the first place. No suicide can expect to get away with total annihilation if they scream before the act itself. Genuine suicides go quietly.

I resume my slog through the obfuscating exhaust mist and decide that I want to get rid of her for once and all.

I tell her quite harshly that she was trying to get attention by screaming that loud.

"It seems like a perfectly reasonable option to me," she spits back at me.

I launch into a moralising speech about how I never try and get anyone's attention. I've got inner resources that mean I don't need to be grovelling pathetically in the underground every time I'm depressed. I am sustained by higher things than people.

"Are you of a religious persuasion?" she asks. There is a hopeful naiviety about her that doesn't tally.

I shake my head and say that I am, except that I worship every God known to mankind. For all her sophistocation, she is mystified. I smile, with a divine twinkle in my eye. I enjoy one of those rare moments of feeling superior to someone.

"So why do you watch all those horribly boring video tapes of people on the Underground?"

"To find out where the Gods are!" I exclaim.

She shakes her head in disbelief. I am quivering under the weight of my revelation. It is the first time I have admitted my true purpose to anyone. She laughs hollowly, clearly unnerved by what I've said. She garbles something that I can't hear or understand properly; she seems to be saying she used to believe in God, but no God would preside over the obscenities she had seen in her life, and not have a damn good go at committing suicide.

As we turn down Swinton Street I tell her that I've got proof that there are numerous Gods.

I feel caught in something of a dilemma. The Map retains its sacredness (and hence its power) by not being seen. I have shown it to no-one. Not that there's been anyone around to see it. I am fully aware that she might completely misinterpret me. She might think that I believe in it all literally. She might fail to understand the metaphorical subtleties of my system.

And yet I want to teach her a lesson. I want to show her that it is possible to survive without having any friends or relatives.

Something in the napalm-like air of the city makes me feel the time has come. The plunge has to be taken. Her complacent depression is indicative of the time we live in. It needs to be broken, so that the planet may realise its true potential.

A feverish desire to be messianic grips me there and then in the godless street. I cock my head at an angle so that my brain soaks in total shadow from the fire-gutted Georgian terraces. I summon up my Aboriginal prayers onto my lips and silently mouth them in front of her. I have become beyond the merely human. A ceremonial fire is raging up through my head.

I grab her by the arms. She flinches and struggles against my tightening grip. She says:

"I could incapacitate you in a second."

And I believe her, but an *Ubermensch* force is guiding my puny body. Her tough, stringy arms relax inside my shaman's lock. I pull her up the rucked, cement steps and shove her onto the dented railings as I open the door. She tilts her head up to the dome-blue skies and opens her mouth as wide as a sunflower petal. She gulps down the sky like someone who is drowning.

I bundle her into the high, decaying grey hall. I push her up numerous, ramshackled flights of bare wooden stairs. She seems frightened but is magnetised by my faith.

I turn the locks on my door. I open it with all the due aplomb and ritual.

Immediately I feel uneasy. The darkness of my room has a different taste than I ever encountered before. There is a hot, lavender aroma curling about in the base of my throat. The darkness almost seems slippery and wet. A slug-like softness sucks against my cheeks. She steps into the room of her own accord, leaving the circle of power I had trapped her in down below. I hear her muted grunts of amazement and feel bitterly disappointed. Her voice seems to resonate, then deaden and shrink from inside the room as if she were caught in a shrivelling womb, an imploding cave.

I shut the door on the daylight and face the sticky, porous darkness.

I am slapped in the face by the glowing map.

It spills and loops its angry, green phosphoresence in wild dimensions over the walls, ceiling and floor giving the impression of limitless length and depth to the room.

There almost seems to be a Biblical wrathfulness in its frenzied activity.

Spitting shadows jut over the huge stalactites and stalagmites that represent the different zones of London. The map-skin is draped in fold after fold, like molten iron, over these mythic pinnacles. The stalactites almost seem to be weeping.

Coiling, fast-forwarded highways and byways zoom through the foggy swamps and marshes in between my peaked mountains.

To my horror I find that the carved, intertwining faces of the Gods are poking out from every nook and cranny. Their bulbous eyes preside sadly, almost tragically over the wrecked tower blocks, red-brick terraces and immaculate office blocks.

The landscape of London dwarfs and dominates them. They look as though they are screaming like she did in the Underground.

They are demanding attention so that they don't wither away.

I look with different eyes, on the world I have dwelt in for so long. I stare at the woman, her red hair illuminated by the phosphoresence, wandering in the glimmering maze. I realise what I have been creating: a modern day version of Plato's Cave, a new model for Dante's Inferno, a fresh world for Hades to reign in. I never intended such evil and neurosis to dwell in my own creation.

I look on in disgust at her.

Far from learning anything, she is revelling in the elaborate fantasy, the sophisticated shadow play I have created! She should not be enjoying it! She is chained down in her mind, loving the shadow play, never appreciating the essential realities! She is failing to see the Gods! She begins touching the sacred worshipping points, the emerging Godheads. She pokes out their eyes, yanking at their stomachs and genitals. I scream at her not to touch anything, but she is wrapped up entirely in humiliating my spiritual world.

I run up to her, but I find that my own world backfires on me. As she hears me screaming and thumping frantically, she begins running deeper and deeper into the labyrinth.

I begin losing sight of her altogether. Erratic flashes and bursting flares sneer and leap up at me, as I stumble across the urban deities. Spectrum colour refracts into my eyes and then contracts into blackness.

Suddenly a trembling, silver film squirts up before everything I see. I find it almost impossible to locate where she is standing. I am losing my balance.

I trample and trip clumsily over my precise, spiritual landscape. Office and tower blocks crumble, surburban gardens are left bombed and cratered and numerous accidents bloody the chartered streets. The pathetic, subjugated Gods and Goddesses moan and whine, clutching their malnourished stomachs, biting their brittle hands. I am so irritated by her I don't care about the havoc I am creating.

I find myself hating the map as it obstructs me more and more from getting to her.

Visions of the London I knew before I constructed the map appear before me. I see its slate roofs and cluttered antennae embracing the drab, exhausted sunlight, glorifying in its soul-lessness, its drabness, its lack of vision and mystery. I see a callous female face which seems to be staring from out of its battered cement precincts. It is her face shooting like an asteroid through the stalagtite maze.

I screw up my eyes to shake off her damning gaze. I clench my fists so hard that my nails pierce the skin. Little trickles of blood smear across my palms. I try and shake the vision out of my head so that I can see her properly. Then I remember that she is actually in my sacred room, mocking its holiness.

She has fled to the very outskirts of London, where Cernunnos the Irish God of the Ocean resides. She crouches against the primitivist effigy I have made for him and giggles maliciously. Her face has caught the eddying lights in such a way to suggest that Medusan snakes are bursting out of her skin. She begins groping with her Gorgon hands at the Outer London boroughs with a sickening lustfulness. The map has become so much part of me that she could be touching my own skin.

As her finger twirls and lightly caresses Leytonstone, my back prickles, the knotted muscles in my shoulders ripple and flex. Her trembling hands over the Peckham council estates are soothing my stomach.

I find my skin bubbling in my tatty clothes. Quivering with anger, I tell her that no art forms have the all-encapsulating nature of the Map. The Map incorporates photography, literature, sacred prayer and scientific formulae.

She laughs. She says life is like living in the bottom of a lake.

I pull her up, my head ablaze with my dying Gods and her aristocratic, psychotic mockery. My eyes swell with tears. I tell her that she is attempting to ruin everything I have created by laughing at me. I yank at her thick coat, my arm lifted, about to strike her on the face.

The greenish light catches the white skin on my hand, as if chopping it off in the darkness.

She leaps up and stands beside me. Our breaths are interweaving. Her eyes have stolen the phosphoresence from my hand and are glowing like a cat's pupils.

I can feel an appalling indignation spiralling up in her. She whispers as though she is being strangled, her face practically pressed against mine:

"Go on, go on, you fine male specimen, you supreme, Nietzchean intellect, go on smash me in, belt me in the stomach!"

She seems to have lost control. She flails her arms, scythe-like, against my skinny stomach. Her pummelling is painful, winding me, directed at the lower regions of my abdomen. She is no longer addressing me. Her words sink into the watery darkness. She presses her sticky cheek against mine, but not like I was a member of the opposite sex. She wraps her arms around me like a worm clinging onto a buffetted fragment of earth in a hurricane.

I feel her melting into me. My hatred of her is dissolving. She pulls me closer into her and starts to erupt into a jerky, diseased sobbing. Her stomach is squeaking with grief. She pulls her arms over my shoulders and presses down on me. I am dragged up and down like a rusty piston against her vibrant body.

Her screams make me love her, whether out of pity or empathy or anything I can't tell. I feel a frightening love diving through me. It's a love that muddies my vision so much that I even decide I love the wretched city that laughs at my Gods. I feel everything becoming so distorted that I can't get a hold on any truth. The map seems to be so unclear, so dark, that I know I need to see things clearly.

I am choking, suffocating for light.

I rush up and tear open the thick, encrusted blackout curtains, with her still clinging desperately onto me.

The sunlight punches in through the grimy windows. The profuse dust from the curtains gathers into airy palls and mushrooms head-first into the jaws of the map.

The conglomeration of classical and modern architecture wither and sag like paintings being swallowed up by the sea. The geometric forms of the Gods and Goddesses droop. All character, even their tragic pathos, leaks like oil, out of their bodies. They cannot endure such scrutiny from the sun.

The map looks like a sludgy mound of litter and clay in the daylight.

The true poverty of my crude etchings are cruelly revealed.

She lets go of me and wipes her muddied face with the back of her hand. I say glumly to her:

"It isn't looking too good, is it?" An accepting sadness lingers on every word. A small, wry smile creeps across her face inbetween tiny, hiccupping sobs. She says: "Oh I wouldn't say that. You've just got to remember that everything goes to Hell."

FRIDGE ART
by Carmel Killin

FRIDGE ART

I live in a shoebox. Some would call it that. I have a view of the cemetery and I smoke Camel cigarettes when I'm in the mood. This seems to be most of the time. I'm not the nervous type. My hair is smoky-coloured and limp when it hasn't been washed, buoyant and blond when it has. I wash my hair once a month with a cheap shampoo. I say this last bit out loud in a fake voice, as if I'm in a television commercial.

I'm smoking a Camel now, matter of fact. Sitting in a warm, grey bath with my knees bent to accomodate the shortness of the tub. It is not difficult for me to imagine myself in television commercials. Taking baths inspires this sort of behaviour, I find. My knee caps are dry peaks.

I've often tried to read in the bath but it's a practise that doesn't work for me. I hate having to admit that. The pages get wet no matter how careful I am. Or the heat and steam send me to sleep leaving any reading matter at the mercy of my collapsed fingers. I've lost whole books this way. Anthony Burgess and William Burroughs have drowned in my bath tub. And a summer edition of *Esquire*. Diving for corpses is too much of an emotional experience. I can't bear the sight of soggy pages. I managed once to resuscitate a collection of Eliot poems but the pages were left scarred and buckled, not beautiful to look at anymore.

I'm thinking of throwing the thing out.

I drag on my Camel. Pull the smoke deep into my lungs.

There's been a small misadventure here this morning. Nothing terribly serious. I presume it's the fire brigade you call in these circumstances. I can't thing who else you'd call. It must be the fire brigade. When I've finished my bath that's what I'll do. Call the fire brigade.

I let the smoke out of my lungs. From a certain angle I'm silhouetted in the weak daylight reflecting off the cemetery. If this isn't a television comercial, tell me what is.

I no longer read in the bath. I smoke instead. It's something I can do without inviting tragedy, something I've become quite successful at. I ash into a plastic yellow duck that glides about my tub without its head. I cut the head off because right from the start I could see its potential as a floating ashtray. I lined its hollow body with tinfoil in a neat and precise manner.

An old boyfriend gave me the duck because he knew how much I liked taking baths. It was the tinfoil that disturbed him, not the headless animal, the tinfoil and the meticulous care I devoted to installing it. Very anal, he said. I don't see him anymore, the old boyfriend.

I put out my cigarette and send the duck up to the taps. It bobs about in this murky sea. My tub. I don't think I'm being overly sentimental when I say it looks happy, my duck.

The water's going cold. I stay in this cramped position and look out across the cemetery. I enjoy the feel of dirty water. Being clean doesn't interest me. These days I only bathe to relax.

My bath is free-standing on curled, stumpy feet and is specially angled so that I can see the tops of gravestones.

I have quite nice legs. They're long, not a bad shape. They

come out first as I attempt to get out of the bath. I swing them over the edge of the tub while the rest of me stays seated. I haul myself out by gripping the sides with both hands. To be honest I've never climbed out of a bath like this before. I can't say what has suddenly possessed me. It's awkward, possibly dangerous. Next time I think I'll go back to my usual way of getting out of bath tubs. Standing up first.

I step into a grimy bathrobe and tramp around in search of a Camel. I don't have far to wander. My shoebox is only two small rooms. Bare floorboards, no central heating. In winter I need about thirty Camels a day. I forget where I put them sometimes. Here we are, half a pack on top of a pile of cassettes. I pull one out, a cigarette, and put it in my mouth.

In my bedroom there's a telephone. If I'm going to do this it has to be now. I go straight in and ring the fire brigade. I'm calm and my fingers are steady. Nine, nine, nine. I get a small thrill from that, it's something I've always wanted to do.

They say they'll be ten minutes.

Water drips down my legs. I'm standing by my bed, looking at my face reflected in the window. Smoking and looking at my face. There's this tiny red pimple on my cheek, just forming. Must have happened over night. Occasionally I get these isolated eruptions. I keep looking at my face, and smoking. I'm thirty-two years old.

Men.

I inhale cigarette smoke, holding it in, noticing small cracks in my lips. Men, I say to myself. I'm not thinking about them, I just say the word. In my head. My lips don't move at all. Men. I let out the smoke.

Actually I *am* thinking about them. It's hard not to. There's one in particular who's been chasing me. He's short. I don't normally go for the short ones. For me, anything under five feet eight is on the short side. This makes me sound like a giant, a colossus, a monolith. I am none of these things. I am six feet and one inch of understated elegance.

I don't mind being chased and this one runs fast. When he catches up he's all sweaty and out of breath and I happen to find this very attractive. He asks me out. A date. Movies, dinner, night clubs – the promise of other worlds fall effortlessly from his lips. I feel uneasy. I don't like going out. It's something I tend to avoid. I say, listen Malcolm, why don't you come round to my place? For dinner. His pupils dilate when I suggest Lobster Provençal.

Malcolm is easily impressed. I discovered this last night. I thought he was going to pass out when I put the plate of steaming lobster in front of him. It took three hours to make, but it's no big deal. I've done this before, loads of times. Other men. I've never seen a such a reaction as Malcolm's .

I move away from the window. My dirty bathrobe falls open. Lost the belt for it ages ago. I go and stand by the bath, my legs press against the cold enamel edge. The water looks almost black. I don't usually empty it until I'm ready for another soak. From a great height because I'm a great tall woman I ash into my duck. This is something else I'm good at. Hardly ever miss.

This room with the bath also functions as my kitchen. It is in fact more of a kitchen than a bathroom. There's a refrigerator, a kitchen sink, an oven, a bench, two wooden stools. And a bathtub. If it wasn't for the tub this would pass for an average kitchen. Most people feel uncomfortable in this room. Without too much trouble I can transform the tub into a table. I do this by covering it with a plank of wood and a cloth. But only when I really have to. I did it for Malcolm and the lobsters. He didn't seem to notice. Most people comment one way or another. But not Malcolm. The taps are still visible at one end so you know it's not really a table. Otherwise the whole setup looks just like a normal kitchen.

I've got an old black Westinghouse fridge, late 50's model, a wide, solid thing. I painted it myself. All its contents, including the rusted racks and plastic drawers, are tiled together on the floor next to the fridge. The fridge itself is in a bad way. Scattered around the base are pieces of lobster shell, tortured bits of rubber, various household instruments. The door is shut.

I go up to the refrigerator and I'm shaking. It's barely noticeable but I can feel it. Sometimes I really surprise myself. I lean down to where the chunky metal handle should be and I speak in a loud voice. It's not shouting, just loud, calm. I say, Are you all right? If anyone were watching it would look as though I were talking to my refrigerator.

I don't even know if he can hear me in there.

I bash the door with my fist, twice, then wait for a response. Nothing. I move back from the fridge. I stare at its black silent shape for a couple of seconds, no longer, then put out my cigarette. Throw the butt into the bath water.

I haven't had a job in a long time. Not a proper one at least. I'm not worried. I'm not the type. Like I said I'm not nervous and I certainly don't worry about not having a proper job. What I mean by proper I don't exactly know.

It's winter. I should be cold wandering about like this but I'm not. I put it down to good circulation. Anyway, the gas heater is on in the bedroom. There's not a lot to occupy my mind, I'm just sort of hanging about. Waiting. Delaying the moment when I'll have to get dressed.

I go back into my bedroom and notice something blue poking

out from under the bed. A pair of almost fresh knickers kicked out of sight last night. Didn't want Malcolm to see. I prefer not to wear knickers at all but if I must – and it's certainly shaping into one of those days – then it may as well be this hardly-used pair.

The simplest thing would be to bend down and pick them up. Or hook them onto my toe and flick them through the air. I do neither of these things. What I do is I fall into a push-up position. My arms collapse almost immediately. I may be tall but I'm not strong, no muscles to speak of.

My face has fallen into my blue knickers. They don't smell *too* bad. Now I can't get up. Don't want to, can't make myself. I like this feel of bare wood beneath me.

I lift my chin and see something I haven't seen in a long time. The space beneath my bed.

No, space is not the right word. There's very little space under there. What I'm looking at is a museum of discarded objects. Forgotten shapes and lumps of things. What a collection.

It's been ages since I was down this way. A year, maybe two. There's a lot of stuff under here. I look at it all, try to take it in. Without thinking too much about it I move my body, not away from the bed but towards it. Forward and under. I slide under my bed on my stomach. Slide on smooth boards, my nose to the ground. I've surprised myself. I didn't know I was going to do this.

It's been a long time all right.

When the fire brigade says they'll be ten minutes I guess that's what you can expect. I've never had to call the fire brigade before. They're bound to be impressed when they see the job I've done on the sealing rubber. I hacked it all out with a pair of nail scissors so that air could get through. They didn't sound over the moon when I told them that on the phone but I know they'll feel differently when they actually see it. When they see the effort it took. I reckon I've saved his life by doing this.

I have crawled further under my bed than intended. Only my toes remain visible. If someone were to come into the room now that's all they'd see of me. I keep on crawling. I slide further in until nothing of my body remains. This is difficult to do because of all the stuff in the way. I have to push things aside. So many things.

I'm not the sort of person who makes lists, I find that kind of behaviour boring. But here under my bed it's exactly what I do. I can't help myself. It's not enough just to look. Names form themselves in my head. I just can't help myself. I start by noting some of the obvious things. My old typewriter, for instance, and a huge fibreglass surfboard that stretches the length of the bed. That's not mine. The suitcase is. And the Wellington boots. The straw hat. These are easy. Big things. A bunch of dead flowers still wrapped in cellophane (can't remember what that was about). And smaller things. A red light bulb, empty cassette cases, one dirty ear plug, dozens of opened letters, four pairs of knickers (including the blue ones), a few loose cigarettes, a fork, a small plastic Godzilla, some crumpled playing cards – a jack of hearts, five of clubs, three of diamonds -

What am I doing? This sort of thing doesn't interest me in the least.

I turn over on my back. Lumps and edges and points of things stick into me. Cellophane, paper, plastic, glass even, make noise under the weight of my body. Everything shifts. It's a weird sensation, though not unpleasant.

I've never seen a man sweat the way Malcolm does. The way he did last night when the lobster came into the room. Certainly it was a beautiful sight, perched on its bed of mussels and crab claws and slimy seaweeds. If it had been me I might have swooned or gasped at the beauty of it but I would never have sweated. Sweating's not something I do naturally. I find it attractive, sure, but still I think it was an odd reaction.

The sweat poured out from under Malcolm's thin hair. It cascaded down his face, his ears, his neck and into his clothing. It flowed into his love-sick eyes and slipped out again like tears. Love-sick. That's the only way I can describe the look on his face. The look that fell upon the orange crustacean as I carried it out across the short distance of the room. I've never seen a reaction like it.

Malcolm is a stand-up comedian. This is what he tells me. He tells me while sucking on his lobster-flavoured fingers. The ruins of dinner are spread across my bath/table. We sit opposite each other, both of us hunch-backed on the wooden stools. He's onto his fifth alcoholic drink, Mexican beer with a thin slice of lime, when he announces it. I look at his purple shirt, his thick neck, then up to his moist, oval face and you know, I believe him. I truly believe him.

I tell him straight away that I don't like comedians. I tell him I don't like jokes, sketches, puns, one-liners, anecdotes, smoky clubs or benefit gigs. In short, I don't like comedy in any shape or form. I lay it on thick because I'm terrified he's going to break out into one of his routines now that he has revealed himself to me. Can you blame me?

The ceiling of my bed is close to my face. I pull a hard edged object out from under my head. A book. W. B. Yeats' *Collected Poems*. Now here's something. I have to admit it, I'm excited. Though you'd hardly suspect it by looking at me. I thought this book had become another bath casualty, had gone the way of the others. Death by saturation. But all this time it's been safe and dry and living under my bed.

I wasn't *really* terrified. I can't imagine anyone being terrified of Malcolm. He has these long eyelashes. I'm tempted to call them beautiful. They're long and perfectly curled at the ends. They seem to weigh down his eyelids, giving him a permanently sleepy look.

Malcolm offered to leave when I expressed my dislike of comedians. I told him he might as well stay. But no comedy. No gags. Nothing even faintly humorous. He accepted this with a nod. I'm not offended, he said. Malcolm I don't care if you're offended or not. I didn't say this, I thought. I sent the message out in the cold stare. There's no way he could have missed my meaning. Malcolm's reply was unexpected. That wasn't real Lobster Provençal, he said.

Comedians bring out the worst in me. I have to say it. Not that I've entertained them in my home before. Not that I've ever had anything at all to do with them. Not until Malcolm. I'm hoping this is a one-off experience.

I know it wasn't Lobster Provençal. I know this. I can't quite believe he's gone to the trouble of pointing it out. Anyone could see it wasn't Lobster Provençal.

I'm a bit peeved. Understandably. I reach for a Camel. I haven't been counting but something tells me I'm nudging past the forty mark. I look across at Malcolm while lighting up and I say, yeah, but it was lobster at least. A beautiful one, he says. Beautiful. I can't argue with that. I want to, but I can't.

If I'd known he was a comedian I would never have let him in the front door.

We talked for eight hours, more or less. I can't believe we had that much to say to each other. But we did.

We drank all the alcohol I had stored in my flat. Six bottles of Corona, a bottle of Bulgarian wine, a bottle of vodka, half a bottle of J&B, a few glasses of cheap port. Awful stuff that port. Plus we drank everything Malcolm had brought – a bottle of cheap white and a duty free litre of Cointreau. He drank a lot more than me. He got pissed quickly. I watched him get pissed. I watched his body slide off the stool, crawl across the floor a short way then prop itself up against the fridge. I propped mine against the bathtub. We were drinking Cointreau, the last of our supplies, when Malcolm started sweating again. It was nearly four o'clock in the morning.

I remember the conversation just before he passed out. You could see where the sweat had travelled to. Malcolm's purple shirt had dark, wet patches. His hair stuck to his head. He wasn't gushing this time. This was more the trickling kind of sweat. More discreet. Very sexy if that's the sort of thing you go for.

It's not surprising I remember the conversation. That lobster again.

Sweating gently against my refrigerator Malcolm, unprovoked, reaveals the ingredients of real Lobster Provençal. Butter, garlic, shallots, tomatoes, thyme and rosemary. Lobster. Chunky bits of lobster meat. Removed from the shell. Flamed in brandy. Cooked gently. Arranged on a bed of boiled rice.

Malcolm looks pleased with himself. It's the most unpleasant sight I've witnessed all evening. I feel the urge to spit at him but something holds me back. This is not like me. How have you become such an expert on lobsters? I ask him. My tone of voice is flat. Malcolm looks at me. He seems to be multiplying small equations in his head, but it's unlikely. You don't want to know, he says. I do want to know, I just asked you. You don't want to know, he says again. Why not? I ask him. Oh god. The most obvious thing I could possibly have said. I hate myself immediately for saying it. Played right into his hands. Malcolm is unbearably smug. He opens his mouth to speak and I notice that his eyes have an unfocused look about them. You said I'm not allowed to be funny, says Malcolm with a weak attempt at a smile. This is a strange kind of answer. I'm about to say something when he slumps to the floor, just like that.

He must be feeling a bit cramped in there by now. Arms and legs getting a bit stiff. Backache, probably. A headache certainly. I'm surprised I haven't heard any banging. That's the first thing I'd do if I woke up and found myself inside a refrigerator. I'd pound the thing with my fists.

There hasn't been a sound since I locked him in.

I pick out two cigarettes from the sea of objects under my bed. I stick one behind my ear, the other in my mouth. But I haven't got a light. Oh, well. I suck on a dirty old Camel and it's him I see. Malcolm.

I am confident he'll be all right. The firemen are on their way. They've got bolt cutters, crow bars, chain saws. I imagine. Everything is under control.

I say I locked him in but it was an accident. Simple and strange. Not difficult to imagine.

It's some small hour in the morning and I'm sucking on my bottom lip, looking at the useless body on my kitchen floor. Malcolm the comedian. I suppose I could drain the tub and deposit him in there for the night. It would be quite comfortable with a pillow and blanket. I dismiss the idea almost as soon as I think of it. Let him lie where he is.

I swallow the last of the Cointreau. May as well. I am wide awake and hungry so I open the fridge door. I can do this without having to shift Malcolm's body. There's nothing to eat in the fridge. By nothing I mean a carton of Parmesan cheese, a bunch of carrots, milk, mustard, celery. Nothing. Malcolm's body at my feet illuminated in the ghastly light of the fridge. I let the door swing open then stand back to get a better look. I switch off the kitchen light. Looking at him sprawled at the foot of my fridge two words come to mind. Spooky and surreal.

On a shelf in my bedroom is a Minolta camera. I set it on a tripod and take seven or eight photographs of Malcolm and the fridge. Each one is different. The contents of the fridge peer down at him from various positions while Malcolm stays the same. The film is 1000 ASA. For one shot I place three crumpled carrots on Malcolm's stomach. I am tempted by other possibilities. Parmesan cheese sprinkled in the hair. Mustard nipples. Rivers of milk slipping down a smooth chest. That sort of thing. My heart beat speeds up noticeably.

Those firemen are sure taking their time.

My body is sprawled on the surfboard at an odd angle and it's not so comfortable. My ear presses up against the fin. It's smooth and cold. I'm trying to remember where this surfboard came from. Trying, but no answers come to me.

I do not smear food into Malcolm's body. I can't bring myself to do it.

For the last photo on the roll Malcolm is huddled in my empty fridge. It was easier than I thought.

First I take everything out. Then I haul Malcolm in, pull him up from the neck. Push his bony chest and shoulders into the space of the fridge. I heave his body up against the back wall until his waist and hips are inside and his head folds down under the freezer box. Then I bend his knees up to his chin. Push and prod a little more, tuck in the sticking-out bits. He's a small man. It's not so difficult.

I take the photo immediately. Hurriedly. As if I'm scared Malcolm will suddenly open his eyes, complain and ruin the shot completely. It's dawn outside the window. The light in the room is perfect. I sit down on the edge of my tub and stare for a long time at what I've created.

Malcolm in the Fridge. I wish there was someone else here to share it with. The photo, if it turns out, will be a poor substitute. I smoke three Camels in a row. What else can I do?

It's funny the way things turn out. The way you do things you never planned on.

I stub out my cigarette. I walk up to the fridge. Malcolm looks cosy and foetal. Safe. I shut the door on him. I didn't know I was going to do that. I honestly didn't. Nor did I imagine what a kick I'd get out of it. Such a simple gesture. Done it a thousand times or more. But this once – so different. How can I describe the feeling? I can't. I can't even let go of the handle. It's only by opening the door that I discover I can breathe properly again. The trouble is I've tasted that delicious feeling and I want more. I want it over and over again. I slam the door shut. I open. Slam. Open. Slam. The floorboards shake from the impact. It is wonderful, glorious. I open the door and now it's me sweating. Malcolm hasn't budged. Well, that's not my fault. It can't be said I didn't give him plenty of chances to snap out of it.

I close my eyes and conjure up a handful of firemen. They should be here by now.

I already have the answers to their questions. The ones I know they'll ask. Like, what is this man doing in your refrigerator? Why did you shut the door? Why is the handle missing? I've got all the answers, I'm not worried.

They will see the instruments I used to try and free him. Left abandoned at the base of the fridge. The snapped broom handle, tools of various descriptions, mangled kitchen utensils, a garden fork. The dints in the fridge door from where I smashed away at it with a hammer will show the impassioned fury of my attempts. I will tell them how I wailed tormented questions into the fridge, receiving nothing but silence for my effort. There won't be the slightest doubt that I didn't try my best and hardest. They will look at all the evidence, they will shuffle it around in their heads, they will use powers of reasoning. Until finally they'll be satisfied. They will see how easy it is for something like this to happen.

There is urgent knocking at my door. Frantic spasms of sound. At last. They seem to have been a lot longer than ten minutes. The knocking becomes louder, more impatient. This surprises me. A fire brigade that panics. Not a good sign.

I crawl out from under my bed. Wrap my bathrobe close to my body and hold it closed with one arm. I catch sight of my reflection in the window. I turn for a better angle. This could well be another television commercial. Belgian chocolates spring readily to mind. I have the taste of them as I make my way to the door. There is nothing particularly hurried or urgent about my movements. To be honest, I would be far from unhappy if they just kicked the door down. Smashed their way in with the soles of their firemen's boots. I know they won't. But it's there at the back of my mind. It would give me a kind of thrill if they did this.

I open the door. There are four of them. They are dressed in immaculate, buttoned uniforms. They have boys' faces, these men, and they are all wearing their helmets. Now there's something I wasn't expecting.

I smile, a rare thing for me.

THE AMBASSADOR

John Mangan

When he had to choose, the Ambassador chose the wrong way. All the gates of the University led down to car parks; only one could claim a close proximity to the Creative Writing Centre.

So, instead, the Ambassador abandoned his car and found himself orbiting the heavy bulk of Sixties British University Brutalism, a grey accretion of concrete so massy it seemed to dent the landscape, making a bowl of earth which seemed to draw the visitor to its lowest point, like a river, running down-hill. A decaying orbit that every minute led him further away from his appointment and closer to the lake.

Yet here, as the ground grew softer, muddier, and the wind lashed up waves he was aware of the most succulent freedom, a freedom compounded of memories of other moments of youthful truency, of unexpected days off school, of days between last exams and last days of term. Adult freedoms could not compare. This freedom opened wide its arms, fraternally embracing the older man and his younger self, bringing them together in a wonder of forgotten ambition and lost ideals, of naivety remem-bered and sophistication achieved.

This time was his own. Not yet late, not yet lost and with a familiar principle of going forward if what lay behind seemed unlikely to yield results. So he walked on around the lake, only stepping out of the way once as a young girl in a white singlet and sweat-soaked grey shorts pounded past, waving a sun-browned hand in thanks.

Now moving uphill behind the runner, the gap widening, he watched the long hair tossing like the wire from the Walkman, heard the susurration of secret music. By the time he was moving past the bookshop, breathing heavily, thighs as heavy as the all-surrounding concrete, the runner was passing out of sight, aimed like an arrow into the watery sun.

The back of the head in the Professor's office was also too young; the hair black, cinched into a tail that swished, crackling with static, in front of a word processor. From notes to screen, from screen to keyboard and back again, the never ending No. The slight movement at the door caused the writer to pause in mid-paragraph and turn.

The Ambassador saw a tall, slim young man, in blue jeans and a plain black sweatshirt, hair pulled back tightly from a smooth high forehead, the green eyes scintillating under some inner sun.

"Sorry. . . didn't hear you," he said.

"No, please. It was not my intention to disturb you", the Ambassador replied. "Far from it. I know how difficult what you are doing is, in both the technical and creative sense."

The Student grinned.

"The Professor said to say he'd be late. I get to use his machine in exchange for doing chores."

"I see," said the Ambassador. "And do I deduce that these chores are not unrelated to the Professor's quasi-mythical aversion to organization?"

The younger man paused, seemed to pass the sentence on some internal screen.

"I guess if you mean the Prof's double-booked himself again, you've got it. You know each other?"

The Ambassador placed his attaché case on the desk.

"We're of the same vintage, you might say. We both attended what turned out to be a kind of Manhattan Project for the Great American Novel at Berkeley, back in the Sixties. It turned out one successful author, a handful of respected writers and myself. Of course, in those days, we used quill pens and half-blind monks illuminated our pages with gold leaf."

The Student inclined from the waist to play a confident arpeggio on the computer's keyboard (like Jerry Lee Lewis, the Ambassador thought, kicking the stool away) saving the text to a small blue disk which he slipped into his shirt pocket.

"Half-blind I can relate to," he said, switching off the screen. "The Prof thought I might wear my courier's hat now and show you the campus."

"He intends being that late?"

"He doesn't ever intend, but he's going to be."

So confident, the Ambassador thought. Were we that confident at that age, or were we merely arrogant? Were we that good, after all? Falling apart, flickering out, like Grail Knights beset with corruption. And the lissome girls with the long straight hair in long velvet skirts we courted in those far-off days of Camelot. We had long hair too and expanded consciousness and we lived in the Global Village. Now all the hippies are as old as generals facing off in the desert.

The Student murmured "Excuse me" and squeezed past the Ambassador to reach the door. For a moment they faced each other, found they had green eyes in common, strong, patrician faces. The hair mis-matched, the Ambassador's fashionable Washington grey to the Student's long black and, just for a moment, the Ambassador was there, facing down an R.O.T.C. major armed only with a flower, surrounded by neat C.I.A. agents with neat Kennedy hairstyles and the button down shirts and the Brooks Brothers suits.

"You O.K.?" the Student asked, hesitating at the door.

The Ambassador's head snapped around.

"What? Yes. Just remembering, with some perspective."

The Student led the Ambassador back to the main glass doors and down the steps.

"The coffee here will cure that. The Brits murder coffee. I guess they never got over Boston."

They strode together past the Chaplaincy, a grey concrete pill-box set at the top of the campus as though to guard the souls of the students from an army of demons or, in more secular times, tanks, and pushed into the coffee lounge.

The Student brought over two plastic cups and settled back with a sigh as the Ambassador crouched forward, sipping at the scaldingly hot coffee.

"You seem to be very much at home here?" the Ambassador ventured.

The Student stretched as he replied.

"I like the place. I know more about it than home."

He shrugged.

"Besides, it's crawling with Americans. I get to show them around for the Prof on a regular basis. If that doesn't put them off, nothing will."

The Student drank his own coffee.

"The coffee here also has medicinal qualities. I forgot to tell you. It cauterizes wounds. You coming into class today?"

The Ambassador brightened.

"It seemed appropriate as, I believe, your subject today is Henry James."

"More appropriate than you think. Hey, here's the Prof."

The Professor pushed past the crowd around the stainless steel coffee machine, his hands in the air as though surrendering, and loped towards the booth, his right hand now outstretched. The Ambassador stood.

"Sam," the Professor said. "I'm supposed to say it anyway but you're looking good. Really."

"Ray," the Ambassador replied. "I'm feeling good, playing hookey."

The Professor sat down. The Student went for more coffee. The Professor looked around.

"No-one with you from The Company?"

"I haven't spotted one yet," the Ambassador replied, reaching for his cup, "but he's here somewhere. I must say, though, any Spook I could spot wouldn't be one I'd want to trust with my life. Maybe your boy there is our man?"

The Professor smiled.

"Our Bobby? Nah. He's too frenetic to be a Sleeper. And he's only just completed the undergrad. Creative Writing course. Three years. . ."

"Ah," the Ambassador nodded.

"Takes you back?" The Professor was probing now.

"Mm."

The Ambassador was craning his head, taking in the lounge. The Professor saw he had placed the ankle of one long leg on the knee of the other, his arms draped across the back of the booth.

In this position the Professor could see the younger Sam, in a Berkeley diner, about to savage a fellow student's writing, like the great American eagle he had become.

"How's Anne?" The Professor broke into the Ambassador's reverie.

"I was just seeing her," the Ambassador said, "sitting in a corner booth in love with Buckminister Fuller and the Doors. She wanted to live in a Navaho tent. Now she's a corporate lawyer in Miami, owns her own condo."

The Professor glanced up as the Student returned, carrying a grey plastic tray.

"Thanks, Bobby." He turned back to the Ambassador. "You always make her sound like a successful failure."

She was. So was he. The kind of people they were now were the people they swore they would never be the day little boys with grown-up toys shot the students down at Kent State. The Suits, the corporate wage-slaves; Straight Society. That way was death, into the heart of the Military-Industrial Complex, a card in the I.B.M. death machine. And when she had said, later, "I don't know you anymore, Sam," he had realised that they had lost those kids years ago and he didn't know her anymore, either.

"Oh, you know," he said airily. "The old hippy in me."

The Professor took a coffee from the Student.

"Sam here had long blonde hair down to his waist, a long moustache like a Viking and an ethnic wardrobe of striking originality and colour."

The Ambassador checked his watch and stood up.

"Now, if only you'd been able to say that about my writing I could have died a happy man. The class is at two? I've got some work still to do on my speech. . ."

They walked back across the bowl of the University, stopping only for a few minutes as the Professor snapped his fingers and raced into the bookshop, emerging with a small, red parcel. The Ambassador watched the Student run up the steps in front of him, two at a time. He watched the muscles on the backs of the thighs and calves, clenching and releasing; the broad shoulders. No effort.

All so easy at that age, the Ambassador thought. We don't know what we have until we lose it and then the wicked, shameful things we do to tempt it back.

Anne in the condo. The lights on but nobody home. Empty apartments in Washington and Paris and London. She was always competitive but, like she said, she liked the competition to be roughly comparable. I cheated her in every sense.

Alone again, the Ambassador turned left and went back down to the lake. In his mind he saw the trails of the three men now exploding and separating, like an Apollo moon shot, saw himself as Challenger falling to the ocean, conscious of approaching doom and the futility of effort, living the longest minutes of a short life.

The cold, west wind howled in over the hill, ruffling his hair and tugging at his tie, coquettish as a wind from America might be. He thought of the coat in the limo, but sat instead on a grey concrete bench that faced the most away from the prows of the concrete warships behind him. Only the B-52 hangar that was really an art gallery touched his eye to the right.

Gusts of cold air grated the surface of the water. Sometimes clear green and deep the lake also seemed to cloud over, advancing a milky opaqueness across its length, as though thrown up by a skater on a curve at Rockefeller Center.

The Ambassador held the round artificiality of the lake in his mind's eye as he tried to read but the words were mantras. Lines of official policy passed again and again before him like the patterns in a lightshow and there it's Jimi Hendrix singing 'Purple Haze' at a San Francisco Happening, running his hand up and down the fret of his Stratocaster and singing, "'Scuse me while I kiss this guy."

And then it's London, pushing over the barriers in Grosvenor Square, and knowing British pigs don't carry guns but the Embassy guards do and burning draft cards in a nice country where that's, at worst, a bad case of littering and keeping your face away from the B.B.C. cameras because you don't want to be recognised by the folks back home.

And there's Anne, grooving in the fountains of Trafalgar Square on New Year's Eve, hugging a girl she's just met, some chick on a Glastonbury trip, and looking at him over her shoulder making sure he's getting the point.

And over it all the war in Indo-China that became Vietnam that led to Cambodia and Year Zero and every little war since, where the Military-Industrial Complex met the Middle Ages and fell over, like the heavy in a Charlie Chaplin movie and where Creative Writing just couldn't be as creative as the language the Pentagon was inventing.

Body Count.

Overkill.

Terminate With Extreme Prejudice.

Pacification.

And My Lai, where language went under the experience because words failed. Where the words had to reduce the experience so people could live with it.

And some of the walking wounded, not mentioned in dispatches; a C.W. unit that never left its eyrie in Berkeley, California. Walking up from the lake, approaching the C.W. Centre, the Ambassador looked up at the concrete cliff and saw a man looking back at him from a second floor window, but it wasn't the Student.

The seminar room was small and ringed with chairs of several academic dynasties. Here the plastic stacking variety of a tight financial year, there the clamshell lattice work fantasies of a forgotten Sixties Corbusier clone. The Professor had bagged a black padded imitation leather swivel job that only lacked switches on the arms to be out of James Bond via Captain Kirk. The Ambassador sat next to him.

A few students sat patiently and nodded as the Professor mentioned their names to the Ambassador. The middle-aged woman with the dyed auburn hair and the big round glasses, like an owl, that was Mrs Barrett, named Elizabeth by cruel parents, giving rise to frequent debates as to whether naming affected destiny or vice versa.

Near the door, that was John Little, another American, short and boyish with spiky blonde hair and a pile of subsidiary texts under his chair.

The Student was not present.

"I was wondering aloud, only yesterday in fact, mentioning your visit, why Britain attracts so many Americans."

The Professor subsided, having spun a conversational frisbee into the room. John Little caught it.

"That's very simple and no secret at all. We're seduced. There's thousands of years' worth of culture here and it drips down like mother's milk. England's an experienced *femme du monde.* Decadent, corrupt, decidedly naughty but she speaks the same language. Paris would be better but Americans speak French like Brooklyn cabdrivers speak English."

"But wouldn't you say it's the duty of American writers, as you must inevitably be, to write about America?" the Ambassador suggested quietly. "Can you escape America or being American?"

"Only by dying," John Little replied, "but that must be the best experience of all, as they save it for last."

And it was the same again. Country Joe and The Fish belting out "Whoopee, we're all gonna die" at Woodstock. Soldiers with peace symbols on their helmets carrying M-16s. A little girl running naked up a track, looking back to where the American napalm blossomed on her village.

John Little was American and death was the ride he hadn't yet got on at Disneyland.

"The Professor considers you a kind of prophet for the Great American Novel." This was Mrs Barrett, smiling archly, surprisingly feral. "Which is fine, in America; perhaps a little limiting in a pure 'writer'."

She indicated the parentheses by wiggling her fingers.

"I can't speak for writers," the Ambassador said. "I don't write anymore."

"Oh, why?" Mrs Barrett began but the bulk of the class arrived then carrying cups and writing pads. The Student arrived last and dropped into the chair John Little had saved for him, next to himself.

The Ambassador was surprised at his own surprise. They were Americans abroad with shared interests, shared hopes, a common pursuit. Nothing more natural than there should be a friendship. Yet still he watched them, their legs crossed towards each other, heads bowed close to each other in rapid whispered conversation. A pen exchanged hands, a scrap of yellow paper; they shared some quiet laughter before settling back. Together they looked at him.

They waited.

"We'd best start," the Professor said and put his unlit pipe away with some regret.

"This is Sam Chambers, whom I told you about yesterday, American Ambassador to Britain and all that. Sam has done C.W. courses at U.C.L.A. and Berkeley so, as he's being interviewed tonight about the war situation, he said he'd like to sit in on today's seminar."

The Ambassador sat with his chin in one hand, watching the Student scribbling on his pad. Was he taking notes already? Was it a late essay? Perhaps writing a story of his own in which the Ambassador had only tangential value? The Ambassador nodded as John Little announced his report on the composition of Henry James' *The Ambassadors* and fell to his study again, watching the veins rise and fall on the back of the Student's hand like the swell of a tide as he covered the page in small cramped handwriting.

He tried to follow John Little's argument on Henry James but he hadn't read *The Ambassadors* since Berkeley and John Little's style grated on him, like listening to a piano where just one note is a semi-tone off. After a while he became aware of waiting for John Little's verbal infelicities with that same sense of rising hysteria.

It wasn't that John Little wasn't brilliant. He was certainly that. He moved from structural analysis to exegesis to critical reception with the smoothness of a Stealth on afterburners. He mined Henry James' other novels with the patient thoroughness of an F.B.I. computer. He knew Henry James' life story like the C.I.A. had a dossier on him.

But still. A word here. A comparison of surprising banality there and the Ambassador knew, as only one no longer concerned with writing could know, that John Little was no writer.

John Little had come to England to sit at the feet of the Masters. He had imbibed the rich red wine of Shakespeare, the sack of Ben Jonson. He had taken chocolate with Pope, coffee with Vanbrugh, taken a little wine at Sheridan's great fireside. He had roistered with Byron, considered hemlock with Keats, supped stout with Joyce.

Drunk with words he reeled, he marvelled, and had no words of his own. Hundreds of years of English Literature had not dripped down like mother's milk to John Little. It had gushed, a lake of milk breached, and John Little, trying to swallow it all, had drowned, his talent washed away in the tides of greatness.

So there he was. Another successful failure. John Little was everything but what he wanted to be. The Ambassador could have sung with sheer vindictive joy.

The Professor stirred, looked at his watch. The Student put his pen away, his notes almost as long as John Little's essay.

"Sam has to go at four so it seems to me we should hear from him first then discuss the paper after the break."

The Ambassador sat up and crossed one ankle over his knee. His arms spread over the back of his chair.

"Ray knows where I am coming from here. I don't think it insults him to say that he was always the most stable of us all. Even at twenty it was the jacket and the corduroy pants and the pipe while we were into kaftans and illegal substances."

The Professor sucked at his empty pipe.

"Yes, but you don't know what I was smoking in those days," he smiled.

"I had my suspic'ns, Ray. So. The idea was that we would all meet in this penthouse on the top of the library at Berkeley and write the Great American Novel or, at least, six Great American Novels. We left History to work out the. . ."

An English boy with blue eyes and country-red cheeks addressed his shoes.

"That sort of sounds, you know, sort of elitist. . ."

The Ambassador nodded.

"It was. It was the time of Camelot. America had to have the best damn missiles, the best damn Moon program and the best damn C.W. courses. And we were the best damn graduates in C.W.; from N.Y.U., U.C.L.A., Chicago. And, you know, Ray's the only survivor because he never tried to write the Great American Novel. He knew he couldn't do it."

The Professor looked up.

"I don't think it's that, Sam. I think I said I had some doubts as to whether it was there to do. . ."

The Ambassador rode smoothly over him.

"Whichever. It didn't get done. You never attempted it and we all failed in the attempt. We're the failures, Ray. Not you."

The students shifted uneasily in their chairs, half hiding their faces behind their fingers.

The Professor rallied enough to murmer:

"That rather, I think, depends on your definition of failure. Ken's first novel was no failure."

The Ambassador turned on him.

"And Ken's second novel? His third? Can anybody here even

name them? Ken's novel is pure Sixties. Everything we wrote is pure Sixties. And the Sixties is all about its own failure."

The Student coughed gently. For a long moment their eyes locked. The green eyes fired.

"Even if that were true," the Student said, "no writer's a failure because he writes about failure. The protagonist of that novel is destroyed but his spirit goes on."

Some of the students were nodding. John Little said, "Right."

And somehow the Ambassador knew he had been fated to come to this. That the argument Berkeley had started would end here, the last battle, as the sun set on the Grail Knights and new Crusaders set sail for the East.

He had a sense of the circles of time that had brought him here, back to rooms like this, discussions like these, another war like that war.

And when he looked at the Student he knew that what he was offering him, the perspective the older man could offer the younger would be rejected, as Sam had rejected it, running down the wrong road the day the world had exploded at Berkeley.

He remembered bars across the chairs in the penthouse, shadow bars cast by the great windows and how they sometimes wavered, swayed, smudged with rain; sometimes torrential rainstorms flinging themselves at the windows like beggars, like refugees from the sea.

When that happened, like it happened then, it was easy to imagine a fury, a tsunami, screaming out of the ravaged East, maws dripping blood and water, howling revenge, screaming dead names from that far away country, the one next to the one run by Yul Brynner.

It rained and it was appropriate. Even in Hollywood, colour

was sunshine, monochrome was rain. And now the notice had come and Sam could do nothing to save him, had no rights to claim, would stand in the rain again to watch the big Hercules transports fly away with boys, fly back with body bags, his among them.

"You seem to be saying you're a failure because you're not a writer."

The Student was advancing to a new position.

"But you're the Ambassador. It's a lifestyle you couldn't have hoped for as a writer."

The Ambassador leaned forward, the rest of the class forgotten.

"I walked out of C.W. because I had a young wife, a child on the way and a conviction that I'd run out of words. I scored the highest marks the Diplomatic Corps had ever seen so maybe I made the right choice at the right time. I wanted to serve my country and I'm still serving her."

"You're not married now."

The Ambassador saw that the Student was looking at his ring finger, the pale band of flesh. He became aware of the weight of the ring on the chain around his neck.

"No. It broke up."

"So you could write now."

The Ambassador leaned back. He spread his wings.

"Let's get this straight. Realise, as I did, most of you are not going to make it as writers because that's the way of the world. It's Chaucer's House of Fame. You can say it's unfair. You might even have talent but you still won't make it. I've seen better men than you go down. I've been there."

Out of the deep silence the Student came on.

"And this joining the Diplomatic Corps? Is that how you got

out of going to Vietnam?"

And how could he explain that to him, images of rain wash-ing across his face, that they would not be going together be-cause his talent exempted him, his country had reserved him for immortality just as lack of talent had destined the other to a young man's death at Phnom Pen?

Reserved to run screaming down the wrong road when the ta-lent died beside the returning Hercules, when Anne guessed the truth, when the marriage died and the arrangements began be-cause there was a child still waiting to be born and life became a novelist's knot and the vision died because the words weren't big enough and the Generals had hijacked the language and there was only one other way, other than the Corps, to escape the body bag and that was to tell the truth and be exempted through shame and disgrace.

"I would have been exempted anyway," the Ambassador said.

"The elite thing," the English boy muttered.

"Perhaps so," the Ambassador smiled, mirthlessly, fero-ciously. "But now I am the Ambassador I'm old enough to un-derstand this novel that has taken up so much of the afternoon. May I?"

The Ambassador held out his hand to the Student. After a moment the Student gave him his copy of *The Ambassadors*. He found the speech at the heart of the book. He looked at John Little.

"You said it was William Dean Howell's remarks reported to James that gave him the germ of his story. But look. James' ver-sion is much longer, much gentler. It's a masterpiece of fatalistic regret."

He moved to the front of the book.

"This is Howell's remark and it drips with envy and the pain of lost youth and opportunity. It has nothing to do with Fate. Howells did this to himself. . . 'Oh, you are young, you are young: be glad of it: be glad of it and live. Live all you can: it's a mistake not to. It doesn't matter so much what you do – but live. This place makes it all come over me. I see it now. I haven't done so – and now I'm old. It's too late. It has gone past me – I've lost it. You have time. You are young. Live!'"

"But you still think we'll fail?" John Little objected.

"I know you will. Life will defeat you. It's too big. James knows that so he urges the illusion of freedom. Live as if you don't know you will fail."

"Strether's line," the Student interrupted, "is the right time is any time that one is still so lucky as to have."

The Ambassador sat quietly. His arms came down from the back of the chair, both feet touched the floor.

"It is the artist's gift," he almost whispered, "to tell the lie that reveals the truth. It is the Ambassador's gift to tell the truth that conceals the lie."

"And Howells was both," the Student replied. "As was Hawthorne. Both writers and diplomats."

"So perhaps it's 'Better late than never'?" the Professor quoted.

"'Better early than late'." The Ambassador flung the counter-quote back. "And now I think I'd better go."

The students did not stand as the Ambassador left the room

The Professor caught up with the Ambassador on the steps.

"Don't be angry with me, Ray," the Ambassador said, looking out over the long shadows. "I haven't had much experience of telling the truth lately. I got a little drunk on it."

"'And what is Truth, said Pontius Pilate'."

The Ambassador put his hands in his pockets and tried to see the lake.

"I haven't forgotten what it is, Ray. There just isn't much call for it anymore. Shall I say we're fighting for democracy or the oil this time? Shall I toss a coin? Does it matter?"

"Truth matters. You said a lot of true things in there, but they hid the big lie. Again."

The Ambassador nodded.

"So I failed. Again?"

The Professor touched his shoulder.

"In there, yes. You didn't get what you wanted. Here."

The Professor took the small red parcel out of his jacket pocket and offered it. The Ambassador took it and, opening it, saw a once well remembered yellow cover.

"Your novel," the Professor said. "Don't lose this one. It takes months to track down these old things."

So long ago, the Ambassador thought. Do I know this writer anymore?

"My only novel," the Ambassador murmured.

"Because you knew the truth then. We all did."

The Professor turned back into the foyer, leaving the Ambassador alone on the steps, turned into the now stinging wind.

Still looking at the book, the Ambassador followed the path of least resistance, let gravity take him, came to himself again beside the lake, now as black as the night it contained, as deep as space.

Looking back he thought he could just make out a figure at the window of the seminar room, long shadows across his face. He decided it was the Student: cast him in the role.

The Ambassador sat on the concrete bench for the rest of the evening, between land and water, earth and heaven, past and future, lies and truth, responsibility and freedom; oblivious to the cold and the pain in his hands, the book in his hands.

In the morning the Ambassador was gone, as though he had never been.

ON THE LINE
by Ian McAuley

I still don't know what it was about that particular night. There was nothing out of the ordinary about it – except, of course, the usual.

Why a small miracle should have happened then, and there, is a complete mystery to me, even though every detail of the night's work remains all too vivid.

It was an ordinary terraced house, distinguished only by its number – eleven. We arrived at about quarter past midnight. There was no doorbell, no door knocker. Only a white, gloss-painted door.

I knocked hard. Once, twice, in quick succession. It's funny how aware one can be of the thickness of paint that seperates the skin of knuckles from the wood of the door.

I paused, just long enough to allow a sleeping head to raise itself from the pillow. I knocked again, once, twice. My heartbeat took up the sense of rhythm, and I was suddenly aware of the way in which my breath was warming the air in front of me. I glanced back at my two colleagues. Adam – young, fresh, and filled with a sense of duty. . .

But no, there are too many details to relate, and they are of a nature no different on this occasion than several dozen others. Suffice it to say that outside that door stood a good team in which I had every confidence, whilst inside, the house stirred. And in due course, the door was opened by one of London's many millions of inhabitants. A man, the father, in his dressing gown, who called down the mother. Subdued with fearful anticipation, they whispered to each other as they led us into the living room.

No-one we call on ever thinks to switch on a side lamp. Which isn't very surprising, but does make for grim atmospherics. And this particular room was already cold with the anonymity of hard-won respectability. Nothing to catch the eye except the open drinks cabinet, and the framed photos of children in their school uniforms. And the parents.

When people asked me about this aspect of my work, I'd say, "It never gets any easier", but that's not really true. A good technique always makes a job easier, and if my technique was now very good, it was still getting that little bit better every time.

And on that night I was immediately faced with a problem that I knew could prove very awkward. The mother had called down her young son, a boy of perhaps eight or nine, and was now holding him close, as if they were posing for a family portrait.

Pausing for a few seconds to shape the right sympathetic but authoritive tone, I said – "I think it would be better if he went to his room, Mrs Evans".

"We're a family, and I want us to be together", she replied defiantly.

I could see it so clearly in her, that basic fear of the human condition – that we are ultimately alone, and that everyone who must suffer must ultimately suffer alone. The fear was surging through her, as ruthless as the sea. She loved the boy, of course, but fear was overwhelming her normal consideration for his well-being.

It was time for some technique. I looked round at the father – an unobtrusive appeal for a second opinion. It worked. The father gave the boy a slight push and the boy gladly ran away up to his room, his mother unresisting.

And now it was all technique.

"Please sit down."

They did.

"I have some bad news for you."

Quickly, quickly, on to the point.

"I'm afraid that your son, Christopher Evans. . ."

– You have to tell them the full name or they'll argue with you, saying that you must have got the wrong person –

". . . is dead."

That's the most important technique of all – get to the point and tell them straight.

The news broken, people usually just stand there, helplessly wanting to do something, but connecting only with the air around them. This couple were no different. So we made our usual moves – Adam put his hand on the father's shoulder, and the WPC held the mother's hand.

It is precisely at this moment that the bringers of the bad news experience what I call 'The Wall'. Which is perhaps not the best of metaphors, but it does for me. It's the sensation you get when you're in the presence of people whose human defences have been stripped away, and the sudden and unexpected death of a young person always does this to the ones who truly loved them.

It's difficult to understand unless you've experienced it, but a person emoting, feeling, without the usual human restraints, exerts an almost physical pressure on you. Quite quickly, you start to become very tired, and before too long you feel totally drained.

I always thought that dealing with this pressure was like having to brace a wall which would callapse if you didn't hold it up. And so I called it 'The Wall'.

'The Wall' is like a feeling of pure love, but expressed through the pain of pure loss. It's raw, it's on the edge of human experience, and it's without doubt the most truthful human expression there is.

That's about as much as I can say.

And so as my colleagues were doing what they could to console the parents, I was standing a little distant, bracing myself against 'The Wall' and waiting for the next question. I always waited for that question – "How did he (or she) die?" – even though I rarely had to wait any time at all. But I always waited, because I believe that they're only ready to hear the answer when they're willing to ask the question.

Perhaps I should stress again that nothing I've described so far was at all out of the ordinary for these occasions. The parents' responses were well within the normal range. Not too hysterical, not too much of the stiff upper lip. Just normal.

But it was just then that I felt this very strange and alarming sensation. I felt myself move. I felt the pressure of 'The Wall' pushing me, pushing me back, back across a line in my mind, a line that I didn't know existed, but it was real, for as I crossed it I was different, I was vulnerable, and I was sharing the pain of the human beings crying on the sofa before me with an intensity that wasn't almost unbearable, it was unbearable. It was terrifying.

I found myself sitting in an armchair and Adam beside me, asking me if I was all right. I wasn't , but that's one of the great things about being a trained professional – your technique will always save you, whatever the crisis.

And so when the parents asked their questions, I gave my answers, and everything continued as per plan. But even as my technique stayed the course, my thoughts were drifting somewhere else altogether. For the force which had opened me up to the people in front of me, had also opened up parts of my memory that felt as musty as any pharoah's tomb.

As I was telling the parents – "It was a hit and run driver" – I was also listening to voices from my past. They weren't insistent, but just drifted by, reminding me of their existence.

One voice in particular comes to mind. It was that of an armed robber I'd once questioned. It was an odd case. His wife had given birth on the morning of the robbery, but he went ahead with the job anyway, exactly as he'd planned it. During the robbery, our man forced a security guard to kneel, put a shotgun to the back of his neck, and blew the top of his head off. No-one had done or said anything to provoke this. Following the killing, several witnesses heard our man chuckle and say – "One comes into the world and one goes out." Under questioning, I asked him if he would have shot the guard if his wife hadn't given birth that day. He chuckled, again, and there was a sparkle of recognition in his eye, as if to say "You're a clever bloke." But you can't put down a sparkle of an eye in a transcript, and all he would say for the record was – "One comes into the world and one goes out." He fancied himself as the philosophical type, and, for him, I suppose, I was just a copper who was clever enough to be able to appreciate it.

And then images started to float before me , all of them images I'd been trying to bury in the dead letter box of memory for years. For a moment I tried to muster the willpower to fight them back down, but like the voices, they weren't insistent, they were just reminding me that they were there. So I let them come.

I'll mention just one. From a sex crime, of course – they're always the worst. It was a diary, written with the clarity and objectivity of a technical manual, and illustrated with what can only be described as diagrams. The author was a modern-day medieval torturer – controlled, unhurried, meticulous, precise. However, it wasn't the confessions of heresy or plot that he was interested in extracting – only pain, terror and humiliation.

And so there I was sitting in the armchair with all these voices and images drifting around me. I remember I was vaguely looking over at the WPC – who was on the phone asking for a doctor to come and adminster sedatives to the mother – when suddenly the whole immense weight of having to deal day by day with the lowest and most disgusting aspects of human behaviour collapsed down on me. How can one person bear so much evidence of human evil, live amongst it so intimately, and yet remain fully human?

And just as suddenly, I realised why it was that I'd always volunteered to do the job of breaking the bad news to bereaved families.

I'd always told myself that since by common consent I was good at it, it was therefore my duty to do it. I radiated a certain mature confidence, a sense that there was still something solid left to hang on to in the world. That's what one of my colleagues once said, anyway.

But for the first time I realised why I really did it. I did it because I needed 'The Wall' as much as any drug addict needs his fix. I needed that injection of pure human love in my life to help counter all the evil that every day weighed so remorselessly in on me.

For this evil was continually pushing me towards a line, a line beyond which one has lost some of those things that make us complete. Beyond that line lies detachment born of defeat, and consolations which can only be bought by bitterness, cynicism and hatred. Beyond that line, one's spirit is already dying.

And I realised then that over the years, only 'The Wall' had stopped me from permanently crossing that line, never to return.

And for some reason that still makes no sense. That night, 'The Wall' created by that very ordinary couple suddenly shoved me so far back from that line that I could feel – what was it? I felt – adolescent. Yes, it was that immensely fresh feeling of an emotional life unblunted by adult experience. It felt – wonderful.

It was a miracle, a small miracle. And there seemed no reason why it should have happened, except for the only reason that there can ever be for a miracle to happen – because somebody desperately needs it.

It was then that the living room gradually came back into focus for me. The father. Struggling to remain in control for the sake of his wife – unable to look at the boy's photo standing on the shelf, but drawn to it by a power that he knew would destroy all self-control. So he looked at the floor. Or over at his wife. The mother. Incoherent with anguish, talking about her son. Talking on and on. An ordinary woman, with ordinary feelings.

'The Wall' was as powerful as ever, but now the pressure of it gave me a tingling sensation like you get when a leg has gone asleep and you force the blood back into circulation. It's not a particularly pleasant feeling, but you know at least that life is returning. And life was returning.

I knew then that I had to grasp this feeling, and by all the powers I had, not let it go. At that moment, all the values by which I'd lived my life – professionalism, duty, the friendship and respect of colleagues – were all suddenly unimportant. Nothing mattered like my feelings.

Much as I felt for the couple there, and I really did feel the purest of compassion (and fiercely guilty gratitude too), I knew I had to get out. Adam was in fact well able to deal with the situation, so I simply told him to take charge, made up some flimsy excuses, and left.

I'd already written my letter of resignation in my head by the time I reached the car. Early retirement, with ordinary feelings. I was a lucky man.

FENCING
by Clare Morgan

Coming out of the garden, Eleanor met him. He was moving between the high walls on either side like a narrow grey shadow. He was hatless, and his hands were suspended rather palely from the cuffs of his coat.

Eleanor thought, "Where is he going?" because the road didn't lead anywhere, and stepped out into the road to ask if he wanted directions. But something about him stopped her, he looked very pale, very tired, and rather untidy, as if he had recently become a tramp. How strange his feet looked, because his shoes were odd! And one of the shoes was dark, with white laces. Eleanor looked at her own shoes which were pinkish and made of soft leather and done up neatly.

She thought she ought to offer him a drink, and said, "Would you like a drink?" and was on the whole surprised when he accepted.

He looked out of place, sitting on the wooden stool in the corner of her kitchen. His hand shook as he took the mug from her. He seemed very tense. But when he began to talk he seemed quite normal, like anybody you might meet, not that she met many people these days, she lived so quietly.

And seeing him sitting there, and hearing him talk in a low voice, drinking occasionally from the mug, attaching his lips to the rim of the mug, disturbing the steady rise of the steam from the surface of the creamy-looking tea so that it shifted sideways and curled over his top lip and up towards his nostrils like the wispy beginnings of a colourless moustache – all this was very pleasant. She would have liked to think that he reminded her of someone, but he was quite unlike anyone she had met before.

He told her that he came originally from America, and his family had been, way back, Scotch-Irish. Eleanor didn't believe him despite the odd, soft, vaguely transatlantic way he spoke, but she didn't interrupt, she like hearing him speak.

"Yes," he said. "My mother came out from County Cork in the 1920's. My mother. Now there was a woman."

Eleanor didn't ask him anything. She would have liked to know why he admired his mother, but she didn't want to interrupt him, she wanted him to go on.

"Yes," he said again, "a fine woman. But of course, she died."

He shifted his weight on the stool and sat up straighter and put the cup down on the sideboard, and all these movements disturbed the general calm of the room, and the air whirled about uncertainly and didn't know which rhythm to settle into, and Eleanor saw how the light which came in through the window overlooking the fields came in at an acute angle and stopped just short of the man's feet, in a mottled patch of shadow.

Eleanor wondered if she should ask what the woman died of, but the man's words stood on their own, had already, it seemed to Eleanor, built themselves into a monument which dominated the room. They sat for a minute in silence. Eleanor warmed the palms of her hands on her mug. The steam from her mug rose slowly towards the ceiling, in a straight line.

"Now there's something," the man said, "when somebody dies. Have you ever killed a chicken?"

Eleanor shook her head. She didn't like killing things. She felt guilty when she stepped on anything. It was dreadful, stepping on something and crushing it and the insides, so bloody or so colourless, sticking to the sole of your shoe.

"No?" the man said, looking at her fully for the first time. It was surprising how bright his eyes were, how the irises looked dense against the whites, which were slightly creamy and impenetrable.

"No. I don't suppose you would have. A woman like you. My mother used to kill chickens. At the bottom of the garden. She'd slip a carving knife down their gullets. At dusk, usually. You couldn't see them looking at you."

Eleanor got up and opened the kitchen window about an inch. The kitchen had been very silent, except for the man's voice, and the silence had made his voice seem like an intrusion, but now the outside came into the kitchen through the opened inch of window, and it surprised Eleanor by sounding like the subdued hum of some vast machine, all the sound blended in together, the keys meshed and the edges of the sounds accommodating each other, the wind, the trees creaking, the grass easing itself to the shifting direction of the wind, the indiscriminate twitter of birds, except for one persistent chaffinch whose repetitive singing punctuated the near air and sawed at the treble nerves of Eleanor's ear.

"That's how it used to sound," the man said. "Quite like that. But more evening-y. You know what I mean?"

Eleanor nodded.

"Yes. Evening-y. I like the evening. Do you like the evening?"

Eleanor nodded. She thought what white hands the man had. She liked men's hands. She put her own hand up to her cheek and smoothed back a piece of hair.

"You live alone here? Don't you get lonely?"

Eleanor was going to answer but the man was looking around the kitchen as if his mind had already moved forward to something else.

"My mother lived alone. She didn't like it very much. She would rather have lived with someone. Wouldn't you rather live with someone?"

He was looking at her again now, with the full, impenetrable look. Eleanor expected to feel uncomfortable, but did not.

"Well. Living with someone. It's not always so good." The man answered himself.

"You get to bickering. Doesn't matter if it's men or women. Bickering. And then there's the question of yourself. All the accommodating. You get to wondering in the end if there's anything left of you."

He looked down at his hands. He seemed to be studying them as if they belonged to somebody else.

"But I wouldn't keep chickens. It's the killing. the killing's really something else."

He had finished his tea, tipped the mug right up and drunk the last dregs, and his raised elbow looked black and angular silhouetted against the window. Eleanor got up and poured him more without asking whether he wanted it.

"But you'd be good for someone," he said as he took the full mug in both hands. "Everyone's good for someone. Even I've been good for someone, in my time. But it doesn't last, that's the thing with it. Doesn't last."

He shook his head and looked out of the window and said, "Well. And your fence needs mending. I suppose you get someone in?"

Eleanor nodded. She was sitting with her back straight and her hands clasped in her lap. She rembered sitting like that at school Services, when she was too young to take Communion. She would wear white ankle socks and black shoes and sit with her ankles crossed and her knees apart, and watch with a kind of dumb awe the brilliant pieces of light which made a mosaic on the altar, sunlight filtering through the azure robes of angels and the bloody skull of the thorn-crowned, dying Christ.

"And what if I was to fix it for you? It'd take maybe half a day. We could come to some arrangement."

Eleanor said he could mend the fence and watched him working on it through the afternoon. He took off his darkish jacket and under it he had on a pale shirt. The shirt was too short for him and as he moved it came out of the waistband of his trousers, and as he bent and straightened she saw intermittently the knots of his backbone exposed.

By the time it got dark, he had still not finished the fence. She looked out of the kitchen window just as the sun went down and saw him silhouetted against the fence, whose edges were trimmed with red now, as though the whole had suddenly caught fire. The man himself, his hair and the crests of his arms – everything seemed to have caught fire.

It was a very red sunset. The kitchen was filled with the redness of it as they sat together at the table and ate. It was strange to see him eat. Later, when she showed him to the bedroom, which was set apart from hers across the landing where the house made an 'L', the sight of him there made everything strange. Her plain white curtains looked ridiculous. Her dried flowers in their terracotta pot seemed absurd.

She lay on her bed and listened to him using the shower and waited for the moon to rise and thought she would never get to sleep. After a while she felt her skin chill and took off her clothes and got under the covers and the sheets felt too cool against her skin. It was impossible to get her pillow in the right position.

Once in the night she woke, thinking she heard a floorboard creak on the landing, but although she listened and listened she heard nothing more, and decided it was just one of those night noises you get in a house which is gradually cooling after a hot day.

She wanted to dream. She nearly always dreamed. Sometimes the dreams were so vivid they made her actual life seem lacking. But tonight, though she wanted to, nothing would disturb the insistent blankness of her mind.

When she woke up she felt very disappointed. The patchwork counterpane on her bed was perfectly in place. The day was pale grey, with a high skein of cloud.

She had half a suspicion that the man would have gone. When she went downstairs the place seemed terribly empty. But when she looked in his room he was still in bed, not asleep, but lying on his side under the sheet, blinking slowly as if he were thinking, looking at nothing but the wall. The single sheet emphasised his thinness. She could make out the bones of his shoulders, and the bony sweep where the ribs begin. His thigh, in outline, was curiously like a child's thigh, angular and with not much substance to it. When she asked him if he wanted breakfast he said,

"No. I've never been much of a one for breakfast." and turned onto his back and stretched and flung his arm out on the pillow so that the white underskin of it showed.

It was quite some time before he came down into the kitchen. He took the tea she offered him and went outside to finish off the fence. He kept his jacket on this morning, the air was so much colder.

In about an hour, the whole thing was finished. Eleanor went out to inspect it, and he showed her how taut the wire was over the tip of the posts, taking her hand and putting her fingers in between the barbs so she could feel for herself. Touching him was unexpected. It confused her, and she stepped back quickly, and retreated into the house.

The man took a long time to tidy up. She watched him from the kitchen, pretending to do the usual things but unable to concentrate, moving restlessly from one thing to the next. The back of her neck felt tense and she frequently rubbed it, and flexed the muscles by nodding and shaking her head.

The fence was really complete. The new stakes and the shiny new wire stood out against the rest, which had weathered. She knew she ought to be pleased, and yet she felt ambivalent. The man came in and said,

"Well. There's your fence. It's a solid job." and washed his hands and forearms at the sink, and made a lot of lather with the soap which he didn't entirely rinse away, but left decorating the sink, like the spume an ebb tide leaves after a storm at sea.

When he went, it was unexpected. She had thought he might ask whether there were any more jobs. He took the envelope with the money, and tore it open carelessly with the side of his thumb, and counted out the money on her kitchen table, and folded the notes around the coins in a tight, square packet, and put the packet down into the bottom of his trouser pocket, and left the ragged envelope in the middle of the empty table.

The bag of sandwiches she'd given him made an ugly bulge in his jacket. He looked somewhat less thin as she watched him walk away from the gate, and down the road between the tall grey walls.

She went back into the kitchen, in which the smell of him was barely detectable, and saw that the window was still open about an inch, and wondered whether she should shut it, but decided to leave it as it was, for the time being at least.

THE GREAT LEONARDO

Erica Wagner

THE GREAT LEONARDO

His heart was pounding now, like it always did just before he went out into the ring. He had imagined he would get used to it: that his palm, curved around the handle of the thin black whip, would cease to sweat, and that his chest would cease to feel constricted by the glittering silver leotard. He had always dusted his armpits with talc; shifting from foot to foot he felt the wet mineral slippery on his skin. He inhaled, flexed his arms, watched the muscle bunch like the back of a dolphin curving through water. Muscle he'd made, a penance, after peering, that first day, into the dim stinking gymnasium that looked a fit place for atonement. It was filled with twisted black and steel machinery, straps and iron weights, racks whereon he could stretch his thin white body into something new. At first, he did not know what to do. He watched the others, would not speak or ask, but saw them buckle their strong shapes into the instruments and pull, push, lift. No one met his eyes, and he was glad. It hurt, and he was glad. Thus was Adam made, he thought, built out of the dust. I will build myself. I will begin again.

It was a cold day, it was February, the first time she came into the church. He remembered her red nose, her red earlobes, and her fingers, when she pulled them out of her woollen gloves, delicate as spines of silver birch. She had opened her purse awkwardly, her cold hands clumsy, pulled out a coin and put it in the wall-box: it clattered loudly for there were so few beneath it. He smiled as he stood at the back of the church, a dust-cloth in his hand, the sleeve of his cassock pushed up; but she did not. She did not see him. She walked quickly to a pew at the back and sat very still, her eyes on the altar, gripping the pew in front of her. She did not remove her coat. After a while she knelt, and leant her forehead on her hands. It was a broad forehead, square and very white, the hair pulled back off her face with a plain black band; an Alice-band, it was called, and she looked like Alice, with her grave face and straight back, her delicate hands and small feet. All these things he had noticed, as he stood by the altar, and found himself thinking it was as if he had never really seen anyone before, as if he had been blind.

But had he? He thought of some of his other parishioners and what they looked like: Mrs Arnold, with her thinning, dyed hair (always a little grey at the roots) and spectacles resting on her bosom, anchored to her body with a thin gold chain; Mark Andrews, his bright face leached of colour by his wife's recent death, towing his three small children dutifully, carefully, as if they might break or be snatched away as his wife had been.

No. He knew them well. And yet here, kneeling at the back of the church on Wednesday afternoon, was a woman he had never before seen and yet in whom he suddenly saw the meaning of the words he had known all his life: *in our image, after our likeness*. He stared at her – her head was still bowed – and held the dust-cloth very tight. Her shoulders rose and fell, a sigh or a sob, he did not know, and then her head came up and she saw him.

He must still have been smiling, for now she smiled back, a tentative, momentary flutter.

He turned and walked quickly into the vestry.

The smell was just the same as when he was a little boy, only stronger. His father used to take him to the circus every year; there was a troupe that came each spring and set up their tent on the village green. It wasn't a very big circus, they didn't have elephants or lions, but it was a circus nonetheless, and he had loved it. There were white horses with sparkling bridles that trotted sedately round the ring while girls with taut, muscular thighs danced easily on their broad backs; there was a trapeze, and a tightrope, and a Polish family who traversed the air above the ring, back and forth, up and down. His father bought him candyfloss and peanuts and they sat rapt, afraid for the Poles and their feats of daring, laughing at the clowns, admiring the horses and the pretty girls. And all afternoon there was a smell of sawdust and sweat, of the horseshit the clowns with their big brooms could never quite clear away, and of people packed too close together, their homes, their lives, all crammed in under the hot lights in the tent. He had loved it. His mother had not liked them to go; she thought it was wicked. She had told him, he ought to confess it on Sunday, confess going to the circus; but he never did. He knew it was not wicked; he did not want to give it away.

His mother was long dead. He could not have faced her now. And yet the circus scent in his nostrils called up her stern face, much easier to remember now she was so far gone. Perhaps she would not even have recognised him with his new, thick brown body, his hair slicked back and his blue eyes rimmed with kohl. This will make you look fierce, Lina had said, leaning over him, the soft black pencil pressed between her fingertips; open your eyes wide, look up. He had looked up high so that he could no longer see her, her white breasts blossoming from her tight sequined bodice. He had blushed, and then thought, it does not matter anymore what I hold in my head, it is all mine.

And the man said, The woman whom thou gavest to be with me, she gave me of the tree, and I did eat.

He began to wonder who she was and where she came from. She visited the church often, but never on Sundays; he had scanned the congregation for her serious face and never saw it. Only in the afternoons, on weekdays, sometimes with a shopping basket over her arm which she would lay down by the door of the church as if it would be a profanity to bring it any farther in. He wondered if it would be; he did not think so. He had never thought of it that way, but was sure that she did.

He did not speak to her for many weeks. He knew that he ought to, for he knew that she was troubled. He was a good priest, a caring priest, and he recognised what he saw in her: her eyes too bright as she gazed at the altar, the fingers white-knuckled, clenched together with wrists pressed down hard on the wooden pew in front. He should go up to her as she stood by the collection-box (she always stood there for a few moments after she had pushed in her coins, indecisive, it seemed, as to whether to go or to stay), touch her arm, say, can I help you, my child?

But he could not. It was not that he was afraid, he could not call it fear; he just – could not. It pleased him when she came in:

when he saw her, he would breathe a sigh of relief. Then he would place himself as far away from her as possible, in the opposite corner of the church, walking quietly, looking over his shoulder to catch glimpses of her bent head. It was clear that she did not wish to speak to him – did not wish to see the priest, he corrected himself. Not yet. He wondered if she would – surely she would – and then wondered what he would do.

He knew nothing about her. Only her little, thin hands, the small feet in plain shoes and slim ankles in thick stockings. He thought they were slim ankles; but he had not much experience of such things. He liked the sound of the two words together: slim ankles. The brown hair pulled back from her forehead, always the same, with the black band, no earrings, no jewellery that he could see. He wondered if she wore a cross at her throat. No make-up. Her face, below the wide, wise forehead, was not particularly pretty; the eyes were deep set and a little too close to the nose for what he knew was considered beauty; but her mouth was kind, relaxed, more relaxed than the rest of her, and a fine rose pink. Peering through the gloom of the church, he thought he could see the faint traces of lines around it; he guessed she was about his age.

He did not think of love, and he did not think of sin. He watched her face as he imagined he would watch the face of the Mother of God, should he ever see it. Her pale skin glowed in the light, in the faint flicker of the candles by which she knelt. He felt wonder.

❖

Across from him, on the other side of the tent, they were rolling out the cages, one by one, linking them together to form a train of ferocity. It was quite dark in the wings, he could not see very clearly, but he could make out the shapes in the cages, moving, twisting in their small spaces, opening their jaws and pressing their fur against the bars. As they came closer to him, the note of the smell changed slightly, darkened with civet. He closed his eyes and inhaled. It was a splendid, dangerous smell, unlike anything else he knew. It was more a texture than a smell, so vividly did it conjure up the feel of thick fur – gold, orange, black, silver-spotted – of the slick blunt teeth and saw-toothed tongues rasping against his skin. He loved this: the hot scent in the moment before they met. He welcomed it, took it gratefully into his lungs. He knew they sensed his presence as much as he did theirs, and it made a vivid bridge between them, across the tent, across the ring, waiting for the moment when they would speak to each other and touch each other. At that moment, when the cages were opened, the ranks of seething, fidgety people became still, watching his glittering smoothness move so easily among the huge beasts. They would think, he has tamed them with his whip and his strength, but he knew that was not so. For in the ring, the love between them grew into a great searing sun that almost singed his flesh, hotter than the fiery hoops through which they leapt at his command. It was not so different from the old love, of incense and altar and velvet; it was only a new mystery. The sweat trickled down between his shoulders as he watched the clowns roll about the ring, run up and down in the dimness of the audience. It was almost time. The ringmaster was adjusting his brilliant coat, pulling on his tie, clearing his throat. In their cages the cats waited.

My God hath sent his angel, and hath shut the lions' mouths, that they have not hurt me.

❖

In the end, of course, she came to confess. He was sitting quietly on the other side of the screen, reading in the half-light, wondering if anyone would come. People rarely did. Yet Mass was well attended; well, times change, he thought. Though it was not so long ago that he was young, and they all went to confession, his friends, his parents, their friends. He had enjoyed it, in a way. He had, in any case, never found it difficult. But then, he reflected, he had never really done anything wrong; and he could recall the priest chuckling as he gave him a few Hail Marys to say. Sin was never something of which he felt he had an adequate grasp. He wondered if that made him a lesser priest.

He was reading the gospel of St. John, because he liked the voice of Christ that he heard in it, human and mystical all at once. That was how he imagined Him. A man you could sit down to dinner with, could laugh with and feel his arm solid around your shoulder, and yet who might at any moment say the most extraordinary thing, the thing that would change your life forever. It might be a little sly, it might be a little riddling, but if you thought hard enough you would come to understand.

If he read this gospel, he thought, he would understand. He read it carefully, moving his lips a little, practically whispering, with the image of the woman – who he now called Mary in his mind – just in front of him, floating in the darkness. The deep eyes were like shadowy beams before him, boring into his flesh and causing him a nameless anguish. He could not find the sin, although he knew it was there. It must be lust, he thought. This is the sin of lust. He tried (he could not do it for very long) to imagine himself and the woman in a room, a room with a bed, where they were naked together, making love. He tried to imagine her voice crying to him, wanting him, and himself hot, burning, as he had been sometimes, pressing his skin against hers, her small breasts beneath his palms. He could go no farther than that. It was not that he felt horror or disgust; he just could not go on. It was not in him. So he thought, perhaps it is not lust: and then the vision of her seemed holy. But he was afraid to discover that lust might wear a cloak of holiness. Michelangelo had painted the serpent with the torso of a beautiful woman. Such things were well known.

I said therefore unto you, that ye shall die in your sins: for if ye believe not that I am he, ye shall die in your sins. Then said they unto him, Who art thou? And Jesus saith unto them, Even the same that I said unto you from the beginning.

The ring-master strode into the ring, long steps in his high shining boots. He was a good man, the ringmaster, a man with faith. His name was Arthur Smith. He had had faith in the hollow-eyed, strong-bodied man who had come to him one day saying he wanted to be a lion tamer. He had not laughed. He had looked down at his big red hands and nodded his head.

"Don't call it that anymore," he had said.

"You don't?"

"No." He looked solemn, appraising. "Don't go down well. This cruelty business. All the fuss. You know. Working with the big cats, that's what we say now. Cat Men, that's what they call them."

"Cat Men."

He had told Arthur Smith that he had been a priest. Arthur Smith did not look surprised, but then, he did not seem the kind of man who would be surprised at anything. He had looked him up and down and then taken hold of his arm and squeezed.

"D'you get muscles like that being a priest?"

"I haven't been a priest for a while," he had said. He did not look into Arthur's eyes.

"Well. Muscular Christianity, I suppose. Why cats, then?"

He said nothing. He had not known. He had only wanted, been certain.

Arthur had been silent for a minute or so. "Funnily enough, we're having a spot of trouble with our man. Don't say I said. Nerves, you know. Happens to the best of them. I like your face. Priest, you say? Go get yourself a broom, man, do a little sweeping. Get a little closer. Take care. See what you think."

It seemed a long time ago, that afternoon. He had told no one else of his previous occupation, and believed that Arthur had kept the information to himself. He discovered that in circuses, people didn't ask. Many of them had grown up in the life and knew nothing else, but the others, drawn from the outside edges of life, appreciated discretion. Slowly, with cautious smiles, they had taken him in. He had, they said, a gift, and gifts they respected. The then Cat Man's nerves got worse, and he started drinking more and more. One morning, he was gone, and he left the glistening leather whip on the bed of the priest.

Now Arthur Smith moved swiftly into the tight circle of white light that swung out to meet him. He raised his hat; swung his arms; smiled, and bowed.

"Ladies and Gentlemen!" he called. "Ladies and Gentlemen! The moment you have all been waiting for! What more can I say? He needs no introduction. Ladies and Gentlemen, I give you The Great Leonardo!"

A little hop off his toes and he was running into the light, his arms wide, his chest wide, his legs pushing him gracefully out into the centre ring, seeing the cages out of the corner of his eye roll to meet him. The clowns and roustabouts pulled the barred train into a semi-circle behind him as he bowed deeply, before and behind, his head nearly brushing the sawdust on the ring floor, his face set still and stern. The crowd – from here they looked like dark bubbles on the surface of turbulent water – shouted and whistled and clapped, twirled their little torches to make small arcs of spinning light.

The Great Leonardo let one arm drop slowly to his side and brought the other hand to his mouth, one finger on his lips, in an exaggerated gesture for silence. There was whispering, shuffling, giggles, and then quiet. He never spoke during the course of his act; the previous Cat Man had been hard of hearing, and had trained the animals with a series of gestures and claps. He had, however, spoken to the audience, told them of dangerous acts of daring, of the extraordinary skill of the animals, warned them of what was to come. The Great Leonardo did not open his mouth.

When he was a priest, his congregation always left the church whispering among themselves. What a beautiful voice he has, they said, so deep and musical. He had always known that this was so. He had liked to hear himself intoning the words of the service, in English, in Latin, letting his sermon (and how well he writes, they said, so simple and clear) roll off his tongue. Like wine in his mouth. He liked to begin his sermons with a reading from the Psalms, simply because he liked to feel the words resound in his head, floating over his palate, ringing the small bones in his ears. *In thee, O Lord, do I put my trust: let me never be put to confusion. Deliver me in thy righteousness, and cause me to escape: incline thine ear unto me, and save me. Be thou my strong*

habitation, whereunto I may continually resort: thou hast given com-
mandment to save me; for thou art my rock and my fortress.

So now that he had escaped, he was silent. He abandoned his
priestly vanity and became a thing of movement only, dwelling
in his body only. It seemed fitting. His self was something entirely new, unrecognisable, and it was right, he thought, that he
should find a new and different voice. And after all, to his real
audience – the great sleek cats – his beautiful solemn voice
would mean nothing at all.

He clapped his hands twice. The roustabouts jumped to the
front of the cages and turned keys in locks, six locks, six doors,
six cages, six cats. The doors opened in a repeating curve, the
roustabouts slipped out of the ring, and the cats glided out of
their cages to sit in a circle around him. The audience began to
applaud, and then, recalling his gesture, rustled quickly into
silence.

There were two tigers, Sheba and Konrad. There were two
leopards, called Silver and Gold because of their coats: Gold a
leopard like any other but Silver seeming bleached and paled,
his spots dark grey against his whitish coat. Orion was a black
panther with knowing eyes like emeralds set in dark velvet. Roland, tawny-bright with powerful shoulders and wide splayed
paws, was a lion. Roland sat at the centre of the circle, looking
out over Leonardo's shoulder. He was smaller than both Sheba
and Konrad, who sat to either side of him, and yet it was he who
commanded the most respect, who made the audience sigh and
shudder. His movements were slow and dignified, and he
seemed to act entirely of his own accord. His mane was thick,
his fur gleaming under the lights. The Great Leonardo stood, a
still centre in the breathing circle of blood and bone. Closing his
eyes, he heard a tail twitching on sawdust, the rasping squeak of

a yawn. He imagined the mouth that made it, peaceful and terrible all at once. Muscle quivered under skin. He raised his
hands high, clapped once, and the circle opened and moved.

❖

The door clicked open; he heard the sound of cloth moving
against cloth, and then the creak of wood as she sat down on the
seat. He knew, straightaway, that it was a woman who had entered the confessional; the anonymity of this office, he had very
swiftly learned, was of a limited kind. Smells, speech rhythms,
breathing patterns, all these were easily recognised. He did try
not to notice such things; but he could not really help it. But he
supposed it was the idea that was important: the small dark box,
the little screen between the sinner and the priest creating a new
identity for both.

He smelled plain soap, and heard a slight sigh. He felt the
pressure of a body leaning against the wood of the confessional;
she would be leaning on his shoulder but for the planks between
them. He recognised nothing, neither movement nor scent. He
was sure it was her. His hands grew cold and he clutched at his
Bible, snapping it shut. She jumped. He swallowed, hoped that
his voice would not break when he had to speak.

"Bless me, Father," she said softly, and stopped. The voice
was nondescript. No accent. Perhaps a little deep, deeper than
he had expected. A little trembling in the 'a' of 'Father,' and
then an anxious pause. He remained silent, waiting for her to
finish the form. His mouth was dry; but he did not wish to clear
his throat. He did not want to frighten her.

"Bless me Father for I have sinned," she began again quickly,
almost running the words together. "It is a long time since my

last confession. . ." The quiet voice trailed off, leaving the threat of tears in the air. He heard her breathing, imagined the harsh surface of her brown wool coat rising and falling too quickly.

What would it be that she had to confess, what sin? He realised, quite suddenly, that he did not want to know. Like lantern slides he saw projected in front of his eyes the images he held of her in his mind: the dark bent head, the narrow shoulders, the luminous eyes (in the darkness of the church he had never learnt their colour) gazing at the altar as if it offered some healing, some answer.

Doubt and confusion struck him like a wave of the sea; he was tossed in the surf, his lungs filling with water, lost between the sand and the sky. He pressed his body against the wooden back of the confessional to stop himself shaking, and gripped his Bible until he began to lose feeling in the tips of his fingers. He did not wish to know her sin, he could not offer her anything, he would not say the right words. He would say to her, come out with me, talk with me, let me see the colour of your eyes, and is your name really Mary? He would ask to hear her speak: *My soul doth magnify the Lord, And my spirit hath rejoiced in God my Saviour. For he hath regarded the low estate of his handmaiden: for, behold, from henceforth all generations shall call me blessed.* He would watch the rosy mouth make the words of Mary over, make them for him. And that would be wrong.

He managed to speak, a little. "I am sorry, my child," he said, and clattered his way out of the confessional, the airless little box, sliding on the stones of the church to reach the vestry where he wrenched his shoulders trying to undo the back buttons on his cassock. He had it over his head, had torn his collar off, before he remembered that he had no other clothes in the church. He stood still in his underpants, shivering in the cold coloured light streaming in through the pretty pointed windows that pierced the thick walls.

His predecessor had called himself Rufus, that was all. And no one had ever called him anything else outside of the ring: it suited him. Rufus had not been a particularly adventurous animal trainer; the act he had devised with his six cats was nothing very unusual: sitting up, rolling over, leaping over each other, jumping through hoops, jumping through flaming hoops. Only the leopards would do that, work with the flames. Rufus had said that tigers had a terrible fear of fire – it had been something to get them to stay in the ring with it – and as for Roland, well, he probably would have done it but he'd never wanted to risk that beautiful mane. The priest, leaning against the cold steel bars of one of the cages, had nodded agreement. He had watched Rufus carefully, had charmed him, had been an acolyte. Had gone out and bought the bottles of gin that Rufus was beginning to need, had not always asked to be reimbursed. They had both known what was happening. It was the only way.

There was little difference between the two men's acts, except for the silence. It is almost impossible to retrain big animals, animals that are not inclined to be trained in the first place: he had seen how difficult it had been for Rufus to make even the tiniest of changes. But The Great Leonardo was never bored or frustrated. He felt such absolute joy at being in the ring, alone, dancing with soft-furred death, leading them quietly through their paces. Feeling their love. There was a moment, near the end of the act, where The Great Leonardo would stand still, at the edge of the ring, as if he had forgotten what came next. He would turn to the audience, shrug. And the cats, arranged on their barrels, would watch him intently, willing him to come forward, or so it seemed. Finally, black Orion would leap from his perch and trot up to him, his thick tail held up like an ink stroke, and butt his head against the hand of The Great Leonardo, the corner of his soft mouth dragging against the skin so that the teeth grazed against his knuckles. He would sit, and look up with his chrysoprastic eyes, the pupils narrowing to slits as they faced the light. He purred. Like a cat by a hearth, he purred, rumbling, thunderous, deep in his throat, and the audience would whisper and ripple. And Ah yes, said the nod of The Great Leonardo. Ah yes; thank you, Orion: and he patted him on the head like a good child. They would trot back together to the centre of the ring, companions. And they were his companions, all of them.

He knew the act so well now that he barely needed to think about it. He could watch it going on before him, and feel the splendour of the animals around him, each a different size, a different texture, affecting him in a different way. It was, he admitted, a sensual pleasure, having them around him, and at first he had felt some guilt. And yet his heart was moved by so great a love for them that he felt it could not be evil. The love filled his body and his mind until everything else, all his past life, vanished utterly, and brought him peace, a peace he had never felt standing in the altar, giving out the bread and wine. Then, he had always been fearful, afraid of he knew not what – until she had come into the church and given a shape to his fear. With his strong arm he raised a silver hoop and watched them leap, Silver, Gold, Konrad, Sheba, Orion, Roland, moving the air around him, with the bending grace of trees in wind and the terrific strength of ocean, sucking the fear from his soul. They were the seven stars in the sky. They were seven alike.

Now he stood at the side of the ring; now Orion came to fetch him, as always. He walked with long, loose-hipped strides, trying to feel that his pace matched Orion's, his fingers just brushing the dark fur. Orion leapt back onto his barrel, and Roland jumped down, coming forward to stand by The Great Leonardo.

It was the end of the act. He had never liked it very much, but the audience did, and so he kept it in; it was easy enough. He leaned forward, and stretching out his arms brought his hands quickly together to his mouth, index fingers raised. Then slowly brought them out to the side again. His gaze was intense: absolute silence. The crowd, a dim sequence of shapes and circles, settled again in their seats. Their torches did not flicker. Their sweet smell hung in the air like a tapestry, woven in with the circus scent, a rich curtain around him. He let one arm drop so it rested on Roland's mane; grasped the fur with his fingers. He lowered himself down to his knees and faced the lion. They were eye to eye.

What did Roland think of his face? He always seemed to be gazing at it just as intently as his trainer stared at him. Roland had eyes the colour of antique gold, flecked with black and brown, and fur the colour of wheat shining in the sun. His broad nose was bent like a boxer's, and the fur there was thin, close over the bone, and scarred with a pattern of scratches like the lines of a map. Thick, wiry whiskers sprouted from beneath the nostrils, quivered in the air. The tongue rasped out, once, revealing the teeth which always protruded slightly – pearls resting on the black lip – to their full length. The yellowing canines were nearly an inch and a half long, and one of them, at the bottom, was gold. Roland was not a young lion. His breath was heavy and meaty, intoxicating. The Great Leonardo reached out, touched the lion under the chin, in the hollow between the bones where the flesh was soft and supple, and the lion opened his mouth wide.

For a second, The Great Leonardo peered into the yawning pinkness of the mouth, a mouth dappled with teeth and shining with saliva. He could see the opening of the throat. Then he shut his eyes, and turning his head a little to the side, slipped it easily into the lion's jaws.

The audience gasped. They always did. Though he could barely hear them; rushing breath surrounded him, and spilled into his ears and nose. He held himself very still, let the teeth scrape gently against his cheek. He reached up and stroked the tawny fur of the neck.

And then someone screamed. He could hear that easily enough: a hysterical, keening note that sounded as if it would tear the tent to pieces. Impossible to tell if it was a man or a woman. He felt the cats become uneasy, shift, grow confused, slope off the barrels and circle. Another scream. Someone else? He could not tell. His hand still on the neck of the lion he went to ease himself gently out, but found the jaws had stiffened. Beneath his palm the lion's pulse quickened, jarring against his own. Breathing. Pushing. A growl. And then he saw her again, her sweet, serious face, more vivid than ever, the eyes (he saw now) a deep sea-blue. Wet with tears, staring at the altar, and himself, trembling with his dust-cloth, hovering at the back of the church, the black cassock burning his body, the collar too tight around his throat, pulled tighter and tighter until he could not breathe, could only watch her staring and weeping, the salt tears beginning to flow down her cheeks. *And at the ninth hour Jesus cried with a loud voice, saying, Eloi, Eloi, lama sabachthani?*

which is, being interpreted, My God, my God, why hast thou forsaken me?

biographies

Peter Bowker was born in Manchester in 1959. He now lives in Leeds where he teaches children with learning difficulties. He has written two crime novels and numerous short stories. He is currently working on a novel about the Nineteenth Century Utopian Robert Owen. His jobs have included managing the Luxette Cinema, bouncing and bacon packing. He has all his own teeth and tries to be polite to creatures larger than himself.

Glyn Brown, ex-secretary, sign writer and motorbike messenger, is a free-lance journalist whose work has appeared in *The Guardian*, *Blitz*, *Melody Maker*, *City Limits* and *i-D*, amongst others. She lives in London with her two cats and her typewriter.

C. D. Clark is on the Screenwriting Course, doesn't read or write short stories, is writing a multi-viewpoint novel, *The Grass Orchestra*, about navigation, heroism, Inuit and Viking cosmology, twins, Zenith and sailing the Atlantic, which she shortly intends to do.

Suzanne Cleminshaw went to Simmons College, Boston, for her first degree. She is now working on a novel.

Judith Condon was born in Norfolk and lives in London.

Robert Cremins was born in Dublin in 1968. He graduated from Trinity College, Dublin with a degree in Modern English and Philosophy. His first published story was in *Icarus*, a T.C.D. literary magazine.

Leena Dhingra was born in India and came to Europe as a small child following the Partition. She has lived, worked and studied in India, England, France and Belgium. Her first novel, *Amritvela*, was published in 1988 by the Women's Press. Her work has also appeared in *Watchers and Seekers* (Women's Press, 1987), *Right of Way* (Women's Press, 1988) and *So Very English* (Serpent's Tail, 1991).

Francis Gilbert was born in 1968, grew up in East London, went to Sussex University and was sent to Coventry as a teacher. He has worked as a labourer on a Northumbrian golf course and a theatre director in Brighton. He is a bit of a sad character and likes playing the piano.

Carmel Killin is an Australian living in London.

John Mangan was born in London of Irish parents. To avoid writing he attended the London Academy of Music and Dramatic Art. After five years as an actor and theatre director he went to University anyway. To avoid studying at University College, London, he started writing again; serious plays for theatre, comedy for radio and T.V. He positively welcomed marriage and fatherhood but failed to avoid all those dismal jobs usually found on old Penguin dustjackets.

Clare Morgan grew up in Wales and now lives in Oxford and London. Her novel, *A Bit of The Other*, is published by Chatto and Windus.

Ian McAuley was born in London in 1958 and graduated from the University of East Anglia in 1981. He has produced the documentaries *Death of A Runaway* and *No Home for Barry* for Channel Four, and has run a film distribution company specialising in Third World films. Writing credits include the non-fiction book *Guide to Ethnic London*, and a short fiction film, *A Grand Opening*, for the Channel Four series *True of False*.

Erica Wagner was born in New York in 1967. She has worked as a stonemason, a cook and a thatcher's apprentice, and has had work published in Britain, Australia and the United States. Perhaps surprisingly, she has no affection for the circus.

❖